PRAISE FOR
Night Hawks

"Johnson, the celebrated novelist, short story writer, screen-writer, and essayist, here combines a finely tuned sense of humor with a desire to probe questions that lie at the heart of a reflective existence. Reading these stories, one feels honored to be in the presence of Johnson's witty philosophical mind, and, not incidentally, stunned by the graceful virtuosity of his sentences. His book is a small treasure, one to be read and considered and reread."

—The New York Times Book Review

"A treasure box."

—Newsday

"Johnson's writing, filled with the sort of long, layered sentences you can get happily lost in, conveys a kindness; a sense that all of us (particularly in 'Occupying Arthur Whitfield' and 'Welcome to Wedgwood') have our own stories."

—The Seattle Times

"Best known for his masterful novels and essays, Johnson wrote this rare story collection over a period of thirteen years—resulting in a masterpiece.... Unflinching in his observations, Johnson ultimately offers a message of empowerment and hope."

—Oprah.com

"Charles Johnson deftly weaves the funny with the philosophical."

—*Lion's Roar*

"A modern master's latest array of glittering tales offers the pleasures and solace of storytelling. It's gratifying to put yourself in the hands of a veteran storyteller who knows what he's doing—and is quietly secure in what he's teaching."

—*Kirkus Reviews* (starred review)

"Arresting . . . These are the indelible moments that show Johnson to be a master of the short form. Highly recommended."

—*Library Journal* (starred review)

"These striking stories from National Book Award–winner Johnson (*Middle Passage*) span a wide range of time periods and cultures but are woven together with a subtle thread of compassion."

—*Publishers Weekly*

"This illuminating collection draws on Johnson's Buddhist faith, African American perspective, and aesthetic sensibilities."

—*Booklist*

ALSO BY CHARLES JOHNSON

Night Hawks

STORIES

CHARLES JOHNSON

SCRIBNER

New York   London   Toronto   Sydney   New Delhi

A Work from the Johnson Construction Co.

Scribner
An Imprint of Simon & Schuster, Inc.
1230 Avenue of the Americas
New York, NY 10020

First Scribner trade paperback edition May 2019

SCRIBNER and design are registered trademarks of The Gale Group, Inc., used under license by Simon & Schuster, Inc., the publisher of this work.

For information about special discounts for bulk purchases, please contact Simon & Schuster Special Sales at 1-866-506-1949 or business@simonandschuster.com.

The Simon & Schuster Speakers Bureau can bring authors to your live event. For more information or to book an event, contact the Simon & Schuster Speakers Bureau at 1-866-248-3049 or visit our website at www.simonspeakers.com.

Interior design by Kyle Kabel

Manufactured in the United States of America

1   3   5   7   9   10   8   6   4   2

Library of Congress Cataloging-in-Publication Data
Names: Johnson, Charles, 1948– author.
Title: Night hawks : stories / Charles Johnson.
Description: New York : Scribner, 2018.
Identifiers: LCCN 2017061759| ISBN 9781501184383 (hardback) | ISBN 9781501184390 (tp)
Subjects: | BISAC: FICTION / Short Stories (single author). | FICTION / African American / General. | FICTION / General.
Classification: LCC PS3560.O3735 A6 2018 | DDC 813/.54—dc23 LC record available at https://lccn.loc.gov/2017061759

"Phoenix Jones" © 2011 by Dean Krippaehne, Louis Torres, Dan Roberts

ISBN 978-1-5011-8438-3
ISBN 978-1-5011-8439-0 (pbk)
ISBN 978-1-5011-8440-6 (ebook)

For my grandson, Emery Charles Spearman

Contents

Find the good and praise it.

—Alex Haley

So the first thing we see about a story is its mystery. And in the best stories, we return at the last to see mystery again. Every good story has mystery—not the puzzle kind, but the mystery of allurement. As we understand the story better, it is likely that the mystery does not necessarily decrease; rather it simply grows more beautiful.

—Eudora Welty,
   "The Reading and Writing
   of Short Stories"

Night Hawks

Introduction

Although I've written ten novels since 1970, and pub-lished four that I felt were most successful in terms of philosophy, artistry, and spirituality, my writing roots are in the short story, beginning in 1965, when I was seventeen and published three stories (one of which I illustrated) in the literary section of my high school's newspaper. Those stories, as juvenilia, are reprinted in a wonderfully rich anthology titled *First Words: Earliest Writing from Favorite Contemporary Authors*, edited by Paul Mandelbaum. The first of those stories, "Men Beneath Rags," is about the irrepressible dignity and humanity of two homeless men. Another, "50 Cards 50," dramatizes the feelings of a boy in Harlem who through black-themed Christmas cards purchased by his mother loses his childhood innocence when he is forced to awaken to the tribal ways adults partition the world along the lines of the illusion of race. And a third story, "Rendezvous," is a kind of shaggy dog tale about how during the Cold War an American astronaut and the Soviet cosmonaut he loves must go to ridiculous lengths for their romantic trysts—on the moon.

When I compare those "first words" to these fictions in my fourth story collection, *Night Hawks,* I realize that in the last fifty-two years my literary sensibilities have not changed a whole lot. Half a century later I still prefer to write and read imaginative stories that deepen my bottomless sense of wonder about the operations of consciousness and this mysterious universe it delivers to us moment by moment; stories that can be deadly serious or completely whimsical, playful and irreverent (I am, after all, an old cartoonist, and love humor and irony) yet also contain a measure of honest hope for the promise of our human species; stories mimetic or fantastic; stories that affirm the heroic struggles and triumphs of people of color; and, finally, stories that emphasize the tantalizing "what if . . ." element that is a mainstay of speculative fiction.

In a magnificent anthology I recommend for all readers and writers, *What Is the Short Story?* edited by Eugene Current-Garcia and Walton R. Patrick, the authors make it abundantly clear that the *tale* has been attractive, as a form, for a very long time—to writers as diverse as Geoffrey Chaucer, Nathaniel Hawthorne, and Washington Irving—and within its long tradition we find other forms of short prose—the sketch, apologue, parable, anecdote, vignette, and fable, to name but a few. In May of 1842, in *Graham's Magazine,* Edgar Allan Poe published a review of Hawthorne's *Twice-Told Tales* entitled "On the Aim and Technique of the Short Story" and in that brilliant essay—as well as in his own work—defined the modern short story as a form distinct from the novel, novella, and other kinds of short prose. Poe asserted that the short prose narrative should require "from a half-hour to one or two hours" to read. Furthermore, he insisted that its writer,

> having conceived, with deliberate care, a certain unique or single *effect* to be wrought out, he then invents such incidents—he then combines such events as may best aid him in establishing this preconceived effect. If his very initial sentence tend not to the outbringing of this effect, then he has failed in his first step. In the whole composition there should be no word written, of which the tendency, direct or indirect, is not to the one pre-established design.

Clearly, most novels cannot be read in two hours or convey but a single emotional effect. Poe stressed the importance of "invention, creation, imagination, and originality." To his demand that *every* word reinforce that overall effect, Poe added in another essay, "The Philosophy of Composition" (1846), that "it is only with the *denouement* constantly in view that we can give a plot its indispensable air of consequence, of causation, by making the incidents, and especially the tone at all points, tend to the development of the intention." And in yet a third essay on Hawthorne, published in 1847, Poe condemned his use of allegory, saying, "If allegory ever establishes a fact, it is by dint of overturning a fiction." What emerged from the theory and practice of this nineteenth-century genius, who has been credited with inventing both the modern short story and the detective story, was a craft that judged all examples of this form's success by their "unity of effect."

Others built upon Poe's insights, among them critic Brander Matthews, who, in his essay "The Philosophy of the Short-Story" (1901), attempted to give an even more precise definition: "the Short-story fulfills the three false unities of French classic drama: it shows one action, in one place, on one day. A Short-story deals with a single character, a single event, a single emotion, or the series of emotions called forth by a single situation."

From Poe's attempt to define a *form* the short story quickly crystallized (some would say "ossified") into a *formula* that enjoyed enormous popularity with the public and popular magazine editors at the turn of the century. Current-Garcia and Patrick make clear that what began in the late nineteenth century as a spirited exploration of a new form quickly degenerated into a rigidly commercial, prefabricated formula—"The kind of story most in demand was fast-paced and action-centered, one which moved rapidly to a sharp climax and exploded in a 'surprise' ending." That calcification was fueled by editors of the 3,300 periodicals in circulation in America by 1885, and the close to forty writing craft manuals published between 1900 and 1930. One of my favorites of these is a truly mechanical approach created in 1928 by William Wallace Cook, who in 1910 wrote fifty-four nickel-and-dime novels, his book on "craft" being titled *Plotto: The Master Book of All Plots,* which had a significant influence on Alfred Hitchcock's early film *The Lodger.*

But readers hungered for this quickly digested new fiction. Indeed, its influence can be seen most clearly in O. Henry's fiction, specifically his story of a classic reversal, "The Gift of the Magi." It is present in the work of black America's first renowned short story writer, Charles Chesnutt (read "The Wife of His Youth"), in W. W. Jacobs's "The Monkey's Paw," and in many of Rod Serling's scripts for the *Twilight Zone.* In other words, so influential and powerful was this *form*-become-*formula* that for many twentieth-century readers it limned the contours of what a short story must *be,* and even today in novels, short stories, motion pictures, television episodes, comic books, and graphic novels, instances of it provide the entertainment values of suspense, surprise, and intensity.

Inevitably, a backlash against the rigidity and predictability of this design had to occur. In his studies on American literature, *The Symbolic Meaning,* D. H. Lawrence was at times savage in his criticism of the way Poe's "philosophy of composition" mechanized the form of the story to such an extent that life's mystery, spontaneity, and vitality were lost. These, of course, were crucial aesthetic aspects that defined Lawrence's own brilliant contribution to the novel and short story. In "Edgar Allan Poe," Lawrence decided that

> Poe is hardly an artist. He is rather a supreme scientist . . .
> He is not sensual, he is sensational. The difference between

these two is a difference between growth and decay . . . As an artist Poe is unfailingly in bad taste—always bad taste. He seeks a sensation from every phrase or object and the effect is vulgar.

For Lawrence, "A tale is a concatenation of scientific cause and effect. But in a story the movement depends on the sudden appearance of spontaneous emotion or gesture, causeless, arising out of the living self." Most of those who rebelled in theory and practice damned the early twentieth-century magazine editors for demanding that short fiction fit such an "artificial" mold. "The very technique of the short story is pathological," Herbert Ellsworth Cory stated in a 1917 article in *Dial*, "and titillates our nerves in our pathological moments. The short story is the blood kinsman of the quick-lunch, the vaudeville, and the joy-ride." Two years earlier, Henry Seidel Canby bemoaned in *The Atlantic Monthly* that

once started, the narrative must move, move, move furiously, each action and every speech pointing directly toward the unknown climax. A pause is a confession of weakness . . . Then the climax, which must neatly, quickly, and definitely end the action for all time, either by a solution you have been urged to hope for by the wily author in every preceding paragraph, or in a way which is logically correct but never, never suspected.

For Canby, and many others, this "formula is rigid, not plastic as life is plastic. It fails to grasp innumerable stories which break the surface of American life day by day and disappear uncaught. Stories of quiet, homely life, events significant for themselves that never reach a burning climax, situations that end in irony, or doubt, or aspiration, it mars in the telling."

These judgments were shared by such fine storytellers as Sherwood Anderson. "As for the plot short stories of the magazines," he wrote in 1924, "those bastard children of De Maupassant, Poe and O. Henry—it was certain there were no plot short stories ever lived in any life I had known anything about." In his own fiction in *Winesburg, Ohio,* Anderson rejected the earlier emphasis on plot-driven storytelling and focused on what he called a form that more organically "grew out of the materials of the tale and the teller's reaction to them."

Put simply, the early nineteenth-century efforts to define the short story, which placed it on its feet as a distinct form, led quickly to senility, and that in turn produced an outcry for reform, specifically for greater artistic freedom, by the 1920s. This revolt against formalism was, of course, pervasive in all the arts after World War I—in poetry's free verse movement, the paintings of Picasso, and the sculpture of Eric Gill.*

Fortunately for us, the aesthetics of the literary rebels of the 1920s and 1930s, some of whom worked in lonely isolation for

* Some material on the evolution of the short story is taken from my essay "Progress in Literature" in *Turning the Wheel: Essays on Buddhism and Writing.*

years and were often misunderstood, carried the day, though in pop culture we are still awash in formulaic fiction. I'm sure their spirit of adventure and freedom—Poe's emphasis, for example, on "invention, creation, imagination, and originality—sank deep into my storytelling DNA when I was a young reader and writer in high school. Yet elements of every phase of the short story's aesthetic evolution, formal and structural (and elements from its predecessors, such as the tale, fable, fabliau, et cetera), can be glimpsed in the stories and novels I've published since 1965.

It's a form I've practiced every year, partly because I love its equation-like elegance and compression, and partly because for nineteen years I've written and performed a new work of short fiction for Bedtime Stories, a reading series I fathered for Humanities Washington to support their cultural and educational programs. That event has nudged me to create new works of fiction I would never have dreamed of doing on my own—stories in second-person, third-person, and first-person (audiences always seem to enjoy the greater intimacy and individuated voices afforded by first-person narratives); tales that stretch from ancient Athens, India, and America's slavery era to modern-day America, Japan, and Afghanistan as well as into the future.

All but one of the stories collected for the first time in this volume (but published individually in other places) were composed for Bedtime Stories and to be read in tandem with other writers within a two-hour time period. Some have received awards, like "The Weave," included in the *2016 Pushcart Prize XL: Best of the Small Presses*; or been anthologized, like "Prince of the Ascetics," which appears in *The Best Buddhist Writing* (2008) and *The Best Spiritual Writing* (2010); and "The Cynic" is reprinted in *The Responsibilities of Rhetoric* (2010).

The one exception is "4189," a future dystopia tale I coauthored with the prolific science fiction writer Steven Barnes for *The Burning Maiden* anthology of horror stories (Vol. I). And, really, this is Steve's story. He, a veteran and endlessly inventive entertainer, provided the meat-and-potatoes—the story idea, characters, and plot. I just added seasoning—a little philosophy and lyricism.

As with my three previous story collections, it is my sincere hope that readers will enjoy these dozen tales in *Night Hawks*, and experience a little bit of the possibilities for wonder and mystery that made me fall in love with short fiction as a literary form so long ago.

—Dr. Charles Johnson
Seattle, Washington
August 2017

The Weave

Three thieves battered through a wall, crawled close to the floor to dodge motion detectors and stole six duffel bags filled with human hair extensions from a Chicago beauty supply store. *The Chicago Tribune* reported Saturday that the hair extensions were worth $230,000.

> —Associated Press news item,
> July 12, 2012

So what feeds this hair machine?

> —Chris Rock, *Good Hair*

Ieesha is nervous and trying not to sneeze when she steps at four in the morning to the front door of Sassy Hair Salon and Beauty Supplies in the Central District. After all, it was a sneeze that got her fired from this salon two days ago. She has a sore throat and red eyes, but that's all you can see because a ski mask covers the rest of her face. As she twists the key in the lock, her eyes are darting in every direction, up and down the empty street, because we've never done anything like this

11

before. When she worked here, the owner, Frances, gave her a key so she could open and straighten up the shop before the other hairdressers arrived. I told her to make a copy of the key in case one day she might need it. That was two days ago, on September first, the start of hay fever season and the second anniversary of the day we started dating.

Once inside the door, she has exactly forty seconds to remember and punch in the four-digit code before the alarm's security system goes off. Then, to stay clear of the motion detectors, she gets down on the floor of the waiting room in her cut-knee jeans, and crawls on all fours past the leather reception chairs and modules stacked with copies of *Spin, Upscale,* and *Jet* magazines for the salon's customers to read and just perhaps find on their glossy, Photoshopped pages the coiffure that is perfect for their mood at the moment. Within a few seconds, Ieesha is beyond the reception area and into a space, long and wide, that is a site for unexpected mystery and wonder that will test the limits of what we think we know.

Moving deeper into this room, where the elusive experience called beauty is manufactured every day from hot combs and crème relaxers, she passes workstations, four on each side of her, all of them equipped with swiveling styling chairs and carts covered with appliance holders, spray bottles, and Sulfur8 shampoo. Holding a tiny flashlight attached to her key ring, she works her way around manicure tables, dryer chairs, and a display case where sexy, silky, eiderdown-soft wigs, some as thick as a show pony's tail, hang in rows like scalps taken as trophies after a war. Every day the customers at Sassy Hair Salon and the wigs lovingly check each other out, and then after long and careful deliberation, the wigs always buy the women. Unstated, but permeating every particle in that exchange of desire, is a profound, historical pain, a hurt based on the lie that the hair one was unlucky enough to be born with can never in this culture be good enough, never beautiful as it is, and must be scorched by scalp-scalding chemicals into temporary straightness, because if that torment is not endured often from the tender age of even four months old, how can one ever satisfy the unquenchable thirst to be desired or worthy of love?

The storage room containing the unusual treasure she seeks is now just a few feet away, but Ieesha stops at the station where she worked just two days ago, her red eyes glazing over with tears caused not by ragweed pollen but by a memory suspended in the darkness.

She sees it all again. There she is, wearing her vinyl salon vest, its pockets filled with the tools of her trade. In her chair is an older customer, a heavy, high-strung Seattle city council-woman. The salon was packed that afternoon, steamed by peopled humidity. A ceiling fan shirred air perfumed with the odor of burnt hair. The councilwoman wanted her hair straightened, not a perm, for a political fund-raiser she was hosting that week. But she couldn't—or wouldn't—sit quietly. She kept gossiping nonstop about everybody in city government as well as the do Gabby Douglas wore during the Olympics, blethering away in the kind of voice that carried right through you, that went inside like your ears didn't have any choice at all and had to soak up the words the way a sponge did water. All of a sudden, Ieesha sneezed. Her fingers slipped. She burned the old lady's left earlobe. The councilwoman flew from her seat, so enraged they had to peel her off the ceiling, shouting about how Ieesha didn't know the first thing about doing hair. She demanded that Frances fire her. And even took things a step farther, saying in a stroke of scorn that anyone working in a beauty salon should be looking damned good herself, and that Ieesha didn't.

Frances was not a bad person to work for, far from it, and she knew my girlfriend was a first-rate cosmetologist. Even so, the owner of Sassy Hair Salon didn't want to lose a city councilwoman who was a twice-a-month, high-spending customer able to buy and sell her business twice over. That night, as I was fixing our dinner of Top Ramen, Ieesha quietly came through the door of our apartment, still wearing her salon vest, her eyes burning with tears. She wears her hair in the neat, tight black halo she was born with, unadorned, simple, honest, uncontrived, as genuinely individual as her lips and nose. To some people she might seem as plain as characters in those old-timey plays, Clara in Paddy Chayefsky's *Marty,* or Laura Wingfield in *The Glass Menagerie.* But Ieesha has the warm, dark, and rich complexion of Michelle Obama or Angela Bassett, which is, so help me, as gorgeous as gorgeous gets. Nevertheless, sometimes in the morning, as she was getting ready for work, I'd catch her struggling to pull a pick through the burls and kinks of her hair with tears in her eyes as she looked in the mirror, tugging hardest at the nape of her neck, that spot called the kitchen. I tell her she's beautiful as she is, but when she peers at television, movies, or popular magazines, where generic blue-eyed Barbie dolls with orthodontically perfect teeth, Botox, and breast implants prance, pose, and promenade through the media, she says with a sense of fatality and resignation, "I can't look like that." She knows that whenever she steps out our door, it's guaranteed that a wound awaits her, that someone or something will let her know that her hair and dark skin are not good enough, or tell Ieesha her presence is not wanted. All she has to do is walk into a store and be watched with suspicion, or have a cashier slap her change on the counter rather than place it on the palm of her outstretched hand. Or maybe read about the rodeo clown named Mike Hayhurst at the Creston Classic Rodeo in California, who joked that "*Playboy* is offering Ann Romney $250,000 to pose in that magazine and the White House is upset about it because *National Geographic* only offered Michelle Obama $50 to pose for them."

Between bouts of blowing her nose loudly into a Kleenex in our tiny studio apartment, she cried that whole day she got fired, saying with a hopeless, plaintive hitch in her voice, "What's wrong with me?" Rightly or wrongly, she was convinced that she would never find another job during the Great Recession. That put everything we wanted to do on hold. Both of us were broke, with bills piling up on the kitchen counter after I got laid off from my part-time job as a substitute English teacher at Garfield High School. We were on food stamps and got our clothes from Goodwill. I tried to console her, first with kisses, then caresses, and before the night was over we made roof-raising whoopee. Afterwards, and for the thousandth time, I came close to proposing that we get married. But I had a failure of nerve, afraid she'd temporize or say no, or that because we were so poor we needed to wait. To be honest, I was never sure if she saw me as Mr. Right or just as Mr. Right Now.

So what I said to her that night, as we lay awake in each other's arms, our fingers intertwined, was getting fired might just be the change in luck we were looking for. Frances was so busy with customers, she didn't have time to change the locks. Or the code for the ADT alarm system. Naturally, Ieesha, who'd never stolen anything in her life, was reluctant, but I kept after her until she agreed.

Finally, after a few minutes, she enters the density of the storeroom's sooty darkness, her arms outstretched and feeling her way cat-footed. Among cardboard boxes of skin crèmes, conditioners, balms, and oils, she locates the holy grail of hair in three pea-green duffel bags stacked against the wall, like rugs rolled up for storage. She drags a chair beneath the storeroom window, then starts tossing the bags into the alley. As planned, I'm waiting outside, her old Toyota Corolla dappled with rust idling behind me. I catch each bag as it comes through the window, and throw them onto the backseat. The bags, I discover, weigh next to nothing. Yet for some reason, these sacks of something as common and plentiful as old hair are worth a lot of bank, why I don't know. Or why women struggling to pay their rent, poor women forced to choose between food and their winter fuel bill, go into debt shelling out between $1,000 and $3,000, and sometimes as much as $5,000, for a weave with real human hair. It baffled me until I read how some people must feel used things possess special properties. For example, someone on eBay bought Britney Spears's used gum for $14,000; someone else paid $115,000 for a handful of hair from Elvis Presley's pompadour, and his soiled, jockey-style shorts went on sale in September 2012 for $16,000 at an auction in England. (No one, by the way, bought his unwashed skivvies.) Another person spent $3,000 for Justin Timberlake's half-eaten French toast. So I guess some of those eBay buyers feel closer to the person they admire, maybe even with something of their essence magically clinging to the part they purchased.

As soon as Ieesha slides onto the passenger seat, pulling off her ski mask and drawing short, hard breaths as if she's been running up stairs, my foot lightly applies pressure to the gas pedal and I head for the freeway, my elbow out the window, my fingers curled on the roof of the car. Within fifteen minutes, we're back at our place. I park the car, we sling the bags over our shoulders, carry them inside to our first-floor unit, and stack them on the floor between the kitchenette and the sofa bed we sleep on. Ieesha sits down on a bedsheet still twisted from the night before, when we were joined at the groin, knocking off her shoes run down at the heels and rubbing her ankles. She pulls a couple of wigs and a handful of hair extensions from one of the bags. She spreads them on our coffee table, frowning, then sits with her shoulders pulled in as if waiting for the ceiling to cave in.

"We're gonna be okay," I say.

"I don't know." Her voice is soft, sinus-clogged. "Tyrone, I don't feel good about this. I can't stop shaking. We're *not* burglars."

"We are now." I open a bottle of Bordeaux we've been saving to celebrate, filling up our only wineglass for her, and a large jam jar for myself. I sit down beside her and pick up one of the wigs. Its texture between my fingertips is fluffy. I say, "You can blame Frances. She should have stood up for you. She *owes* you. What we need to do now is think about our next step. Where we can sell this stuff." Her head twitches back in reflex when I reach for one of the wigs and put it on her, just out of curiosity, you know. Reluctantly, she lets me place it there, and I ask, "What's that feel like? A stocking cap? Is it hot?"

"I don't know. It feels . . ."

She never tells me how it feels.

So I ask another question. "What makes this hair so special? Where does it come from?"

Hands folded in her lap, she sits quietly, and, for an instant, the wig that pools her face with obsidian tresses makes her look like someone I don't know. All of a sudden, I'm not sure what she might do next, but what she *does* do, after clearing her throat, is give me the hair-raising history and odyssey behind the property we've stolen. The bags, she says, come from a Buddhist temple near New Delhi, where young women shave their heads in an ancient ceremony of sacrifice called taking *pabbajja*. They give it up in order to renounce all vanity, and this letting go of things cosmetic and the chimera called the ego is their first step as nuns on a path to realizing that the essence of everything is emptiness. The hair ceremony is one of 84,000 Dharma gates. On the day their heads were shaved, they kneeled in their plain saris, there in the temple naos, and took 240 vows, the first five of which were no killing, no lying, no stealing, no sexual misconduct, and no drinking of alcohol. They didn't care what happened to their hair after the ceremony. Didn't know it would be sewn, stitched, and stapled onto the scalps of other people. But Korean merchants were there. They paid the temple's abbot ten dollars for each head of fibrous protein. After that, the merchants, who controlled this commerce as tightly as the mafia did gambling, washed the hair clean of lice. From India, where these women cultivated an outward life of simplicity and an inward life free from illusion, the merchants transported their discarded dead hair halfway around the planet, where it was cannibalized as commerce in a $9 billion industry for hair extensions devoted precisely to keeping women forever enslaved to the eyes of others.

As she explains all this, Ieesha leaves her wine untasted, and I don't say anything because my brain is stuttering, stalling on the unsyllabled thought that if you tug on a single thin strand of hair, which has a life span of five and half years, you find it raddled to the rest of the world. I didn't see any of that coming until it arrived. I lift the jar of wine straight to my lips, empty it, and set it down with a click on the coffee table. When I look back at Ieesha, I realize she's smiling into one cheek as if remembering a delicious secret she can't share with me. That makes me down a second jar of Bordeaux. Then a third. I wonder, does the wig she's wearing itch or tingle? Does it feel like touching Justin Timberlake's unfinished French toast? Now the wine bottle is empty. We've got nothing on the empty racks of the refrigerator but a six-pack of beer, so I rise from the sofa to get that, a little woozy on my feet, careening sideways toward the kitchenette, but my full bladder redirects me toward the cubicle that houses our shower and toilet. I click on the light, close the door, and brace myself with one hand pressed against the wall. Standing there for a few minutes, my eyes closed, I feel rather than hear a police siren. My stomach clenches.

Coming out of the bathroom, I find the wig she was wearing and the weaves that were on the coffee table burning in a wastebasket. Ieesha stands in the middle of the room, her cell phone pressed against her ear.

"What are you doing?" Smoke is stinging my eyes. "Who are you talking to?"

Her eyes are quiet. Everything about her seems quiet when she says, "Nine-one-one."

"Why?"

"Because it's the right thing to do."

I stare at her in wonder. She's offered us up, the way the women did their hair at the temple in New Delhi. I rush to draw water from the kitchen sink to put out the fire. I start throwing open the windows as there comes a loud knock, then pounding at the door behind me, but I can't take my eyes off her. She looks vulnerable but not weak, free, and more than enough for herself. I hear the wood of the door breaking, but as if from a great distance because suddenly I know, and she knows, that I understand. She's letting go all of it—the inheritance of hurt, the artificial and the inauthentic, the absurdities of color and caste stained at their roots by vanity and bondage to the body—and in this evanescent moment, when even I suddenly feel as if a weight has been lifted off my shoulders, she has never looked more beautiful and spiritually centered to me. There's shouting in the room now. Rough hands throw me facedown on the floor. My wrists are cuffed behind my back. Someone is reciting my Miranda rights. Then I feel myself being lifted to my feet. But I stop midway, resting on my right knee, my voice shaky as I look up at Ieesha.

"Will you marry me?"

Two policemen lead her toward the shattered door, our first steps toward that American monastery called prison. She half turns, smiling, looking back at me, and her head nods: *yes, yes, yes.*

Prince of the Ascetics

Once upon a time, my companions and I lived in the forest near the village of Uruvela on the banks of the Nairanjana River. We were known far and wide as five men who had forsaken worldly affairs in order to devote ourselves completely to the life of the spirit. For thousands of years in our country, this has been the accepted way for the Four Stages of Life. First, to spend the spring of one's youth as a dedicated student; the summer as a busy householder using whatever wealth he has acquired to help others; the fall as an ascetic who renounces all duties at age fifty and retires into the forest; and the goal of the winter season is to experience the peace and wisdom found only in the Atma (or Self), which permeates all parts of the world as moisture seeps through sand. My brothers in this noble Fourth Stage of tranquillity, which we had just entered, were Kodananna, Bhadiya, Vappa, and Assajii. We had once been family men, members of the Vaishya (trader) caste, but now owned no possessions. We lived, as was right, in poverty and detachment. We wore simple yellow robes and fasted often.

Wheresoever we walked, always in single file, Vappa, a small man with a snout-like nose, took the lead, sweeping the ground before us with a twig-broom so we would not crush any living creatures too small to see. When we did not leave our ashram to make alms rounds for food in Uruvela, we satisfied our hunger with fruit, but not taken off trees; rather we gathered whatever had fallen to the ground. Each day we wrote the Sanskrit word *ahum* or "I" on the backs of our hands so that we rarely went but a few moments without seeing it and remembering to inquire into the Self as the source of all things. People throughout the kingdom of Magadha affectionately called us *Bapu* (or father) because they knew that we had just begun the difficult path described in the *Vedas* and *Upanishads*. The scriptures say that a fast mind is a sick mind. But we, my brothers and I, were slowly taming the wild horses of our thoughts, learning the four kinds of yoga, banishing the ego, that toadstool that grows out of consciousness, and freeing ourselves from the twin illusions of pleasure and pain.

But one day it came to pass that as we made our monthly rounds in the summer-gilded village, begging for alms, the merchants and women all looked the other way when we arrived. When Assajii asked them what was wrong, they apologized. With their palms upturned, each explained how he had already given his monthly offering to a stunning young swami, a *mahatma,* a powerful *sadhu* who was only twenty-nine years old and had recently crossed the River Anoma, which divided our kingdom from the land of the Shakya tribe. They said just being in his presence for a few moments brought immeasurable peace and joy. And if that were not shocking enough, some were calling him *Munisha,* "Prince of the Ascetics."

"How can this be?" My heart gave a slight thump. "Surely you don't mean that."

A portly merchant, Dakma was his name, who was shaped like a pigeon, with bright rings on his fingers, puffed at me, "Oh, but he *is* such. We have never seen his like before. You—*all* of you—can learn a thing or two from him. I tell you, Mahanama, if you are not careful, he will put you five lazybones out of business."

"Lazybones? You call *us* lazybones?"

"As your friend, I tell you, this young man gives new meaning to the words *sacrifice* and *self-control.*"

Needless to say, none of this rested happily on my ears. Let it be understood that I, Mahanama, am not the sort of man who is easily swayed, but whatever serenity I had felt after my morning meditation was now gone, and suddenly my mind was capricious, like a restless monkey stung by a scorpion, drunk, and possessed by a demon all at the same time.

"This *sadhu,*" I asked, helplessly, "where might we find him?"

Sujata, the unmarried daughter of a householder, with kind, moonlike eyes, stepped forward. "He lives at the edge of the forest by the river where the banyan trees grow. I have never seen *any* man so beautiful. Everyone loves him. I feel I could follow him anywhere . . ."

Now I was in a mental fog. There was a dull pounding in my right temple as we trekked forthwith at a fast pace back into the forest. Vappa was sweeping his twig-broom so furiously— he was as angry and upset as I was—that billowing clouds of dust rose up around us, and we must have looked, for all the world, like a herd of enraged, stampeding elephants. Soon enough we tracked down the brash young man responsible for our alms bowls being empty.

The villagers had not lied. We found him meditating naked, except for a garland of beads, in a diagonal shaft of leaf-filtered light from the banyan tree above him. Straightaway, I saw that his posture in meditation was perfect, his head tilted down just so, leaving only enough space that an egg could be inserted between his chin and throat. He was twenty years younger than I, no older than one of my sons, his body gaunt and defined, his face angular, framed by a bell of black hair. As I glanced between his legs, I noticed that his *upastha* was twice the size of my own. He looked up when we approached, introduced ourselves, and pressed him to explain how he could have the nerve to install himself in *our* forest. In a sad, heavy way he exhaled, holding me with eyes that seemed melancholy, and said:

"I seek a refuge from suffering."

"Who," asked Bhadiya, cocking his head to one side, "are your teachers? What credentials do you have?"

"I have studied briefly with the hermit Bhagava. Then with Ālāra Kālāma and Udraka Rāmaputra, who taught me mastery of the third and fourth stages of meditation. But," he sighed, "neither intellectual knowledge nor yogic skills has yet led me to the liberation I am seeking."

I felt humbled right down to my heels. Those two venerated teachers were among the greatest sages in all India. Compared to *them*, my own guru long ago was but a neophyte on the path.

Twilight was coming on as he spoke, the blue air darkening to purple the four corners of the sky. A whiff of twilight even tinctured the shadows as he unfurled what I surmised was a bald-faced lie, a fairy tale, a bedtime story so fantastic only a child could believe it. Until a year ago, he said, he had been a prince whose loving father, Shuddodana, had sheltered him from the painful, hard, and ugly things of the world. The palace in which he was raised, with its parks, lakes, and perfectly tended gardens, gave you a glimpse of what the homes of the gods must look like. He was raised to be a warrior of the Shakya tribe, had a hundred raven-haired concubines of almost catastrophic beauty, and ate food so fine and sumptuous even its rich aroma was enough to sate a man's hunger. He said he would have continued this voluptuous life of pleasure and privilege, for he had all that this world could offer, but one day while he and his charioteer, Channa, were out riding, he saw a man old and decrepit. On a different day he saw a man severely stricken with illness. On the third day he saw a corpse being carried away for cremation. And when he recognized that this fate awaited *him*, he could not be consoled. All satisfaction with the fleeting pleasures of his cloistered life in the palace left him. But then, on a fourth trip, he saw a wandering holy man whose equanimity in the face of the instability and impermanence of all things told him that *this* was the life he must pursue. And so he left home, abandoning his beautiful wife, Yashodhara, and their newborn son, Rahula, and found his lonely way to our forest.

Once he had breathed these words, my companions begged to become his disciples. Kodananna even went as far as to proclaim that if all the scriptures for a holy life were lost, we could reconstruct them from just this one devoted ascetic's daily life. He had seduced them with his sincerity for truth seeking. I, Mahanama, decided to remain with my brothers, but, to be frank, I had great misgivings about this man. He came from the Kshatriya caste of royalty. Therefore he was, socially, one *varna* (or caste) above us, and I had never met a member of royalty who wasn't smug and insensitive to others. Could only *I* see his imperfections and personal failures? How could he justify leaving his wife and son? I mean, he was not yet fifty, but he had forsaken his responsibilities as a householder. True enough, his family was well taken care of during his absence, because he was a pampered, upper-caste rich boy, someone who'd never missed a meal in his life but now was slumming among the poor, who could shave his waist-long beard, his wild hair, take a bath, and return to his father's palace if one day the pain and rigor of our discipline became disagreeable. I, Mahanama, have never had an easy life. To achieve even the simplest things, I had to undergo a thousand troubles, to struggle and know disappointment. I think it was then, God help me, that I began to hate *every* little thing about him: the way he walked and talked and smiled, his polished, courtly gestures, his refined habits, his honeyed tongue, his upper-caste education, none of which he could hide. The long and short of it was that I was no longer myself. Although I consented to study with him, just to see what he knew, I longed, so help me, to see him fail. To slip or make a mistake. Just *once*, that's all I was asking for.

And I *did* get my wish, though not exactly as I'd expected.

To do him justice, I must say our new teacher was dedicated, and more dangerous than anyone knew. He was determined to surpass all previous ascetics. I guess he was still a warrior of the Shakya tribe, but instead of vanquishing others all his efforts were aimed at conquering himself. Day after day he practiced burning thoughts of desire from his mind and tried to empty himself of all sensations. Night after night he prayed for a freedom that had no name, touching the eighty-six sandalwood beads on his *mala* for each mantra he whispered in the cold of night, or in rough, pouring rain. Seldom did he talk to us, believing that speech was the great-grandson of truth. Nevertheless, I spied on him, because at my age I was not sure any teacher could be trusted. None could meet our every expectation. None I had known was whole or perfect.

Accordingly, I critically scrutinized everything he did and did not do. And what struck me most was this: it was as if he saw his body, which he had indulged with all the pleasures known to man, as an enemy, an obstacle to his realization of the highest truth, and so it must be punished and deprived. He slept on a bed of thorns. Often he held his breath for a great long time until the pain was so severe he fainted. Week after week he practiced these fanatical austerities, reducing himself to skin, bone, and fixed idea. My companions and I frequently collapsed from exhaustion and fell behind. But he kept on. Perhaps he was trying to achieve great merit, or atone for leaving his family, or for being a fool who threw away a tangible kingdom he could touch and see for an intangible fantasy of perfection that no one had ever seen. Many times throughout those months together we thought he was suicidal, particularly on the night he made us all sleep among the dead in the charnel grounds, where the air shook with insects, just outside Uruvela. During our first years with him he would eat a single jujube fruit, sesame seeds, and take a little rice on banana leaves. But as the years wore on, he—being radical, a revolutionary—rejected even that, sustaining himself on water and one grain of rice a day. Then he ate nothing at all.

By the morning of December seventh, in our sixth year with him, he had fallen on evil days, made so weakened, so frail, so wretched he could barely walk without placing one skeletal hand on Bhadiya's shoulder and the other on mine. At age thirty-five, his eyes resembled burnt holes in a blanket. Like a dog was how he smelled. His bones creaked, and his head looked chewed up by rats, the obsidian hair that once pooled round his face falling from his scalp in brittle patches.

"Mahanama," he said. There were tears standing in his eyes. "You and the others should not have followed me. Or believed so faithfully in what I was doing. My life in the palace was wrong. This is wrong too."

The hot blast of his death breath, rancid because his teeth had begun to decay, made me twist my head to one side. "There must be . . ." he closed his eyes to help his words along—"some Way between the extremes I have experienced."

I kept silent. He sounded vague, vaporish.

And then he said, more to himself than to me, "Wisdom is caught, not taught."

Before I could answer he hobbled away, like an old, old man, to bathe, then sit by himself under a banyan tree. I believe he went that far away so we could not hear him weep. This tree, I should point out, was one the superstitious villagers believed possessed a deity. As luck would have it, the lovely Sujata, with her servant girl, came there often from the village to pray that she would one day find a husband belonging to her caste and have a son by him. From where we stood, my brothers and I could see her approaching, stepping gingerly to avoid deer pellets and bird droppings, and, if my eyes did not deceive me, she, not recognizing him in his fallen state, thought our teacher was the tree's deity. Sujata placed before him a golden bowl of milk porridge. To my great delight, he hungrily ate it.

I felt buoyant, and thought, *Gotcha*.

Vappa's mouth hung open in disbelief. Bhadiya's mouth snapped shut. Kodananna rubbed his knuckles in his eyes. They all knew moral authority rested on moral consistency. Assajii shook his head and cried out, "This woman's beauty, the delights of food, and the sensual cravings tormenting his heart are just too much for him to resist. Soon he will be drinking, lying, stealing, gambling, killing animals to satisfy his appetite, and sleeping with other men's wives. Agh, he can teach us nothing."

Disgusted, we left, moving a short distance away from him in the forest, our intention being to travel the hundred miles to the spiritual center of Sarnath in search of a better guru. My brothers talked about him like he had a tail. And while I cackled and gloated for a time over the grand failure of our golden boy, saying, "See, I *told* you so," that night I could not sleep for thinking about him. He was alone again, his flesh wasted away, his mind most likely splintered by madness. I pitied him. I pitied all of us, for now it was clear that no man or woman would ever truly be free from selfishness, anger, hatred, greed, and the chronic hypnosis that is the human condition. Shortly after midnight, beneath a day-old moon in a dark sky, I rose while the others slept and crept back to where we had left him.

He was gone, no longer by the banyan tree. Up above, a thin, rain-threaded breeze loosed a whirlwind of dead leaves. It felt as if a storm was on its way, the sky swollen with pressure. And then, as I turned to leave, seeking shelter, I saw faintly a liminal figure seated on kusha grass at the eastern side of a bodhi tree, strengthened by the bowl of rice milk he had taken, and apparently determined not to rise ever again if freedom still eluded him. I felt my face stretch. I wondered if I had gone without food so long that I was hallucinating, for I sensed a peculiar density in the darkness, and the numinous air around him seemed to swirl with wispy phantoms. I heard a devilish voice—perhaps his own, disguised—demanding that he stop, which he would not do. Was he totally mad and talking to himself? I could not say. But for three watches of the night he sat, wind wheeling round his head, its sound in the trees like rushing water, and once I heard him murmur, "At last I have found and defeated you, *ahumkara,* I-Maker."

At daybreak, everything in the forest was quiet, the tree bark bloated by rain, and he sat, as if he'd just come from a chrysalis, in muted, early morning light, the air full of moisture. Cautiously, I approached him, the twenty-fifth Buddha, knowing that something new and marvelous had happened in the forest that night. Instead of going where the path might lead, he had gone instead where there was no path and left a trail for all of us. I asked him:

"Are you a god now?"

Quietly, he made answer. "No."

"Well, are you an angel?"

"No."

"Then what are you?"

"Awake."*

That much I could see. He had discovered his middle way. It made me laugh. These rich kids had all the luck. I knew my brothers and I would again become his disciples, but this time, after six long years, we'd finally be able to eat a decent meal.

---

* These six lines of dialogue are from the spiritual teachings of the late, great Eknath Easwaran.

The Cynic

The ruler of the world is the
Whirlwind, that has unseated Zeus.

—Aristophanes, *The Clouds*

If you listen to those who are wise, the people who defended my teacher at his trial before he was killed by the state, they will tell you that the golden days of our city were destroyed by the war. The Corinthians, who feared our expansionist policies and growing power, convinced the Spartans to make war against us. Our leader, Pericles, knew we were stronger at sea than on shore. So he had all the inhabitants of Athenian territory in Attica huddle inside the fortifications of the city, which left the lands of the rich to be ravished by our enemies. But Pericles believed that after this sacrifice of land to the bellicose Spartans, our swift and deadly ships, *triremes* outfitted with three banks of oars, would wear them down in a war of attrition. His plan, this gamble, might have worked. But at the outset of the Peloponnesian War, a plague fell upon Athens, laying waste to those crowded together in the city, and, if that was not bad enough, Pericles himself died the following year. With his death, power in the Assembly was seized by demagogues like the young general Alcibiades, who convinced the voters to abandon our defensive strategies and launch an attack on the city of Syracuse in faraway Sicily. This ill-advised invasion, this poorly planned military adventure, drained the manpower and treasure of the *polis,* our city-state. Within two years of the Sicilian expedition, "the hateful work of war," as Homer might put it, had wiped out our ships and ground forces. However, this was just the beginning of the spell of chaos cast upon us by the goddess Eris.

The war dragged on for another ten years, dividing the population, feeding our disenchantment with civic life. Just as the chorus in a Sophoclean drama is powerless to stop the events leading to tragedy, so, too, no one could stop the growing hatred of the poor for the rich, or the bitterness in those wealthy families who experienced catastrophe as they lost their crops year after year. The rich began to plot against the regime, against rule by the people, and against the Assembly, which had conducted the war like a dark comedy of miscalculations and decisions based on collective self-delusion.

When our defeat finally came, after a demoralizing twenty-seven years of conflict, everyone knew this was the end of the empire, that we had unleashed the furies, and entered a time of dangerous extremes, a long-prophesied Iron Age. Crime, fraud, and violence increased. Many Hellenes started to feel that the gods like Zeus and Athena were mere fictions, or were helpless to affect our lives, and that the gossamer-thin foundation of laws and traditions our fathers and forebears had lived by (especially our devotion to *sophrosyne*, or moderation) were arbitrary. The faith in a moral order that unified us during our Golden Age was no longer possible. It seemed that overnight loyalty to our sea-girt city-state reverted back to family, tribe, and clan, and a new breed of citizen was born. These were cold, calculating, and egotistical men like the character Jason that Euripides created in *Medea*. They were devoted not to civic duty but instead to the immediate pleasures of food, drink, sex, and, most important of all, power. These new men, who believed might was right, like Thrasymachus, saw "justice," "honesty," and "loyalty" as ideas created by and for the weak. Not too surprisingly, a new level of nastiness, incivility, and litigation entered our lives. Of these new men, Thucydides said,

> The meaning of words had no longer the same relation to things, but was changed by them as they thought proper. Each man was strong only in the conviction that nothing was secure. Inferior intellects generally succeeded best. For, aware of their own deficiencies and feeling the capacities of their opponents, for whom they were no match in powers of speech and whose subtle wits were likely to anticipate them in contriving evil, they struck boldly at once.

Now, such new men needed new teachers, those who were very different from the wonderful man who taught me. These teachers, foreigners, sprang up like Athena from the head of Zeus, came from places like Corinth and Ceos, were called Sophists, and for a nice purse of drachmae, they instructed the children of the rich in clever, honey-tongued rhetoric and perfumed lies aimed at appealing to the mob and swaying the members of the factious Assembly—prostitutes, my teacher called them, because he charged no fee. The most famous of these men was Protagoras, who argued that everyone knew things not as they are but only as they are in the moment of perception for *him*. "Man," he said, "is the measure of all things," and by this popular saying he meant nothing was objective, all we could have were opinions, and so each citizen was now his *own* lawgiver. (And, as you know, opinions are like assholes—everybody has one.) In my youth, then, at this hour in history, in the wreckage of a spiritually damaged society, it came to pass that common, shared values had all but vanished, truth was seen as relative to each man, if not solipsistic, and nothing was universal anymore.

But the greatest, most unforgivable crime of my countrymen was, if you ask me, the killing of my teacher over his refusal to conform to the positions taken by different political parties. His accusers—Anytus, Meletus, and Lycon—called him an atheist, a traitor, and a corrupter of youth. Then they brought him to trial, and I shall remember for all my days what he said in his defense:

Gentlemen, I am your grateful and devoted servant, but I owe a greater obedience to God than to you . . . I shall go on saying, in my usual way, my good friend, you are an Athenian and belong to a city that is the greatest and most famous in the world for its wisdom and strength. Are you not ashamed that you give your attention to acquiring as much money as possible, and similarly with reputation and honor, and give no attention or thought to truth and understanding and the perfection of your soul?

He could have fled the city, escaping injustice with the help of his students. Instead, and because he could not imagine living anywhere but Athens, he chose to drink the chill draft of hemlock.

To this very day, I regret that I could not be at my teacher's side when he died. That evening I was sick. But since his death, which wounded us all, I have done everything I can to honor him. Being one of his younger students, never his equal, I always feel like a son whose father has died too soon. Right when I was on the verge of maybe being mature enough to actually say something that might interest him. Sometimes I would see or hear something I wanted to share with him, only to realize he was gone for the rest of *my* life. For years now I've carried on dialogues with him in my head, talking late at night into the darkness, saying aloud—perhaps too loud—all the things I wanted to tell him, apologizing for things I failed to say, often taking *his* part in our imaginary conversations until my five slaves, who are like family to me, started looking my way strangely. I didn't want anyone to think I had wandered in my wits, so I began quietly writing down these dialogues to free myself from the voices and questions in my head, adding more speakers in our fictitious conversations, where his character is always the voice of wisdom, which is how I want to remember him. Yet and still, his death left a scar on my soul, and a question that haunts me day and night: How can good men, like Socrates, survive in a broken, corrupt society?

There was one man who seemed as bedeviled by this dilemma as I was, but his response was so different from mine. I can't say we were on the same friendly terms as Damon and Pythias, though sometimes he did feel like a brother, but one who infuriated me because he said my lectures at the Academy were long-winded and a waste of time. He was not, I confess, my only critic. My teacher's other students think my theories are all lunacy and error. They see my philosophy about eternal Ideas existing beyond the imperfections of this shadowy world as being nothing more than my cobbling together the positions of Heraclitus, who saw only difference in the world and denied identity, and Parmenides, who saw identity and denied the existence of change. In their opinion, I've betrayed everything Socrates stood for. They positively hate my political view that only philosopher-kings should rule. Antisthenes has always been especially harsh toward me, treating me as if I was as cabbage-headed as one of the residents of Boeotia, perhaps because he, and not I, was present at Socrates' side when he passed away. Years ago, he had his own school before joining ours. In his teachings he rejected government, property, marriage, religion, and pure philosophy or metaphysics, such as I was trying to do. Rather, he preached that plain, ordinary people could know all that was worth knowing, that an ordinary, everyday mind was enough. He taught in a building that served as a cemetery for dogs. Therefore, his pupils were called cynics (in other words, "doglike"), and among the most earthy, flamboyant, and, I must say, scatological of his disciples was the ascetic Diogenes.

For an ascetic, he was shamelessly Dionysian, and without an obol or lepton to his name; but besides being Dionysian and shameless, Diogenes was a clown with hair like leaves and tree bark, gnarled rootlike hands, and eyes like scars gouged into stone. He made a virtue of vulgarity, wore the worst clothing, ate the plainest porridge, slept on the ground or, as often as not, made his bed in a wine cask, saying that by watching mice he had learned to adapt himself to any circumstance. Accordingly, he saw animals as his most trustworthy teachers, since their lives were natural, unself-conscious, and unspoiled by convention and hypocrisy. Like them, he was known for defecating, urinating, masturbating, and rudely breaking wind in public. He even said we should have sex in the middle of the marketplace, for if the act was not indecent in private, we should not be ashamed to do it in public. Whenever he was praised for something, he said, "Oh shame, I must be doing something wrong!" Throughout Athens he was called The Dog, but to do him justice, there *was* a method in his madness. For example, his only possessions were his staff and a wooden bowl. But one afternoon Diogenes stumbled upon a boy using his hands to drink water from a stream. Happily, he tossed his bowl away, and from that day forward drank only with his bare hands.

Thus things stood in postwar Athens when one day The Dog decided to walk around the city holding a lighted lantern. He peered into all the stalls of the marketplace, peeked in brothels, as if he had lost something there, and when asked what he was doing replied, "I'm looking for an honest man." His quest brought him to the Academy, where I was lecturing. As I placed several two-handled drinking cups before my students, I could from the corner of one eye see him listening, and scratching at dirt in his neck seams, and sticking his left hand under his robe into his armpit, then withdrawing it and sniffing his fingers to see if he needed a bath. I sighed, hoping he'd go away. I turned to my students and told them that while there were countless cups in the world, there was only one *idea* of a cup. This idea, the essence of cupness, was eternal; it came before all the individual cups in the world, and they all participated imperfectly in the immortal Form of cupness.

From the back of the room, Diogenes cleared his throat loudly.

"Excuse me," he said, "I can see the cup, but I don't see cupness *any*where."

"Well"—I smiled at my students—"you have two good eyes with which to see the cup." I was not about to let him upstage me in my own class. Pausing, I tapped my forehead with my finger. "But it's obvious *you* don't have a good enough mind to comprehend cupness."

At that point, he sidled through my students, put down his lantern, and picked up one of the cylices. He looked inside, then lifted his gaze to me. "Is this cup empty, Plato?"

"Why, yes, that's obvious."

"Then"—he opened his eyes as wide as possible, which startled me because that was a favorite trick of my teacher—"where is the emptiness that comes before this empty cup?"

Right then my mind went cloudy. My eyes slipped out of focus for a second. I was wondering how to reply, disoriented even more by the scent of his meaty dog breath and rotten teeth. And then, Diogenes tapped my forehead with *his* finger and said, "I believe you will find the emptiness is *here*." My students erupted with laughter, some of them even clapping when he, buffoon that he was, took a bow. (That boy from Stagira, Aristotle, who was always questioning me, and expressed the preposterous belief that the ideas must be *in* things, laughed until he was gasping for breath.) "I think your teacher's problem," he told them, "is that he'd like to run away from the messiness of the world, to disappear—*poof!*—into a realm of pure forms and beauty, where everything has the order and perfection of mathematics. He's a mystic. And so—so dualistic! He actually wants certainty where there *is* none."

"What," I said, "is wrong with *that*? Things are terrible today! Everyone is suing everyone else. There's so much anger and hatred. No one trusts anyone anymore!"

Again, his eyes flew open, and he winked at my students, raising his shoulders in a shrug. "When have things *not* been terrible? What you don't see, my friend, is that there are only two ways to look at life. One, as if nothing is holy. The other, as if *every*thing is."

Oh, *that* stung.

All at once, the room was swimming, rushing toward me, then receding. I felt unsteady on my feet. In a matter of just a few moments, this stray dog had ruined my class. Now my students would always tap their heads and giggle when I tried to teach, especially that cocky young pup Aristotle. (I think he'd like to take my place if he could, but I know that will never happen.) I began to stutter, and I felt so embarrassed and overwhelmed by his wet canine smell that all I could say was "In *my* opinion, only a fool would carry a lantern in the daytime. Why don't you use it at night like a sensible man would?"

"As a night light?" He raised his eyebrows and bugged out his eyes again. "Thank you, Plato. I think I like that."

There was nothing for me to do except dismiss my students for the rest of the day, which The Dog had ruined. I pulled on my cape and wandered through the marketplace until darkness came, without direction through the workmen, the temples of the gods, the traders selling their wares; among metics and strangely tattooed nomads from the steppes who policed our polis; past the theater where old men prowled for young boys whose hair hung like hyacinth petals, and soldiers sang drinking songs, all the while cursing Diogenes under my breath, because the mangy cur was right. He was, whatever else, more Socratic than Socrates himself, as if the spirit of my teacher had been snatched from the Acherusian Lake, where souls wait to be reborn, and gone into *him* to chastise and correct me from the beyond the grave, reminding me that I would always be just an insecure pupil intoxicated by ideas, one so shaken by a world without balance that I clung desperately to the crystalline purity and clear knowledge of numbers, the Apollonian exactitude and precision of abstract thought. Where my theories had denied the reality of our shattered world, he lapped up the illusion, like a dog indifferent to whether he was dining on a delicacy or his own ordure.

Tired, I finally decided to return home, having no idea how I could summon up the courage to face my students. And it was when I reached the center of town that I saw him again. He was still holding high that foolish lantern, and walking toward me with a wild splash of a smile on his face. I wanted to back away—I was certain he had fleas—or strike him a blow for humiliating me, but instead I held my ground and said crisply, "Have you found what you're looking for yet?"

"Perhaps," he said, and before I could step back, he lifted my chin with his forefinger and thumb toward the night sky. "What do you see? Don't explain, *look*."

It was the first night of a full moon, but I hadn't noticed until now. Immediately, my mind started racing like that of a good student asked a question by his teacher. As if facing a test, I recalled that when Democritus tried to solve the mystery of the One and the Many, he said all things were composed of atoms, and Thales believed that everything was made of water, and Anaximenes claimed the world's diversity could be reduced to one substance, air. Oh, I could plaster a thousand interpretations on the overwhelmingly present and palpable orb above us, but at that moment something peculiar took place, and to this day I do not understand it. I looked and the plentitude of what I saw—the moon emerging from clouds like milk froth—could not be deciphered, and its opacity outstripped my speech. I was ambushed by its sensuous, singular, and savage beauty. Enraptured, I felt a shiver of desire (or love) rippling through my back from the force of its immediacy. For a second I was wholly unconscious of anyone beside me, or what was under my feet. As moonlight spilled abundantly from a bottomless sky, as I felt myself commingled with the seen, words failed me, my cherished opinions slipped away in the radiance of a primordial mystery that was as much me as it was the raw face of this full-orbed moon, a cipher so inexhaustible and ineffable it shimmered in my mind, surging to its margins, giving rise to a state of enchantment even as it seemed on the verge of vanishing, as all things do—*poleis* and philosophical systems—into the pregnant emptiness Diogenes had asked me to explain. A sudden breeze extinguished the candle inside his lamp, leaving us enveloped by the enormity of night. There, with my vision unsealed, I felt only wonder, humility, and innocence, and for the first time I realized I did not have to understand, but only to *be*.

All I could do was swallow, a gulp that made The Dog grin.

"Good." He placed one piebald paw on my shoulder, as a brother might, or perhaps man's best friend. "For once you didn't dialogue it to death. I think I've found my honest man."

Kamadhatu: A Modern Sutra

(FOR MARTIN HUGHES)

The body is the Bodhi Tree;
The mind is like a bright mirror standing.
Take care to wipe it all the time.
And allow no dust to cling.

—Shen-hsiu

Not far from Osaka, deep in the forest, there is a fourteen-hundred-year-old Buddhist temple called Anraku-ji, which in Japanese means "peaceful, at ease." But the young priest who took over the care and upkeep of Anraku-ji not long ago, Toshiro Ogama was his name, felt neither truly peaceful nor at ease, and having said something as puzzling as that, it is now necessary, of course, to tell you why.

When Toshiro Ogama was fifteen, both his parents were killed in an automobile accident in Kyoto. An only child, he was suddenly an orphan. His parents' funeral, conducted by a priest in the Pure Land tradition, and their cremation were engraved into the emulsion of his memory. At the

49

crematorium, they were incinerated at 800 degrees centi-grade. Their bodies burned steadily for two hours. They had a thirty-minute cooling-down period. Finally, their bones were crushed and mixed with the ashes—all total his parents each weighed two pounds at the end—and they were given back to Toshiro in two white urns. Those containers, which he kept and placed beside the altar at Anraku-ji, led him all his adult life to listen attentively whenever he heard the Buddhist Dharma or teachings. And what more? Well, he was pain-fully shy and, like the English scientist Henry Cavendish, he could barely speak to one person, never to two at once since four eyes looking at him made Toshiro stammer. At eighteen, he entered Shogen-ji Monastery and devoted four years to rigorous training, living on a prison diet of cheap rice and boiled potatoes in bland soup. He later passed his examinations at Komazawa University, where many Soto Zen monks have studied, but after this Toshiro decided he did not want to teach or try to work his way up through the politically treacherous Buddhist hierarchy and rigid, religious pecking order in Japan, which was brutally competitive and had corrupted the Sangha, or community of spiritual seekers, by the greed and hypocrisy of the world—or at least this was what Toshiro told himself since he was unable to speak to anyone about his real Zen fears, and why he sometimes felt like a failure, an outright fraud. Knowing he didn't have the family connections or the constitution to rise very high in the religious power structure, Toshiro chose instead to take a free-lance job translating best-selling American books for Hayakawa Shobo, a publishing company in Tokyo, and he looked around for an abandoned temple that he might repair, manage, and perhaps turn into his own private sanctuary from suffering and all the unpredictable messiness of the social world. Across Japan, there are thousands of these empty wooden buildings falling into disrepair, full of termites and rats, with tubers growing through the floorboards, as if each was a vivid illustration of how everything on this planet was so provisional, with things arising and being unraveled in a fortnight, a fact that Toshiro meditated on deeply, day and night, since the death of his parents.

So when he was granted permission to move into Anraku-ji, the young priest felt, at least for his first year there, a contentment much like that described by Thoreau at Walden Pond. He had no wealthy parishioners or temple supporters paying his salary. Whatever he did at the temple was voluntary, with no strings attached, paid for by his translation work, and done for its own rewards. With great care, he spent a year remodeling Anraku-ji's small main hall and adjoining house, quietly chanting to himself as he worked. He pruned branches, sawed tree limbs, and raked leaves. He trimmed bushes, did weeding and transplanting, and drifted off to sleep to the sound of crickets, bullfrogs, and an owl that each night soothed him like music. Sometimes he talked to himself as he worked, which was a great embarrassment when he caught himself, so he kept a cat to have something to talk to and cover up his habit. He was alone at Anraku-ji, but not lonely, and he decided a man could do far worse than this.

Thus things stood when one afternoon a pilgrim from America arrived unannounced on the steps of his temple. This did not please Toshiro at all because, traditionally, the Japanese do not like surprises. She was a bubbly, effervescent black American about forty years old, with an uptilted nose, a smile that lit up her eyes behind her gold-framed, oval glasses, and long chestnut hair pinned behind her neck by a plastic comb. At first, Toshiro felt ambushed by her beauty. Then he had the uncanny feeling he should know her, but he wasn't sure why. In Japanese, he said, *"Konnichiwa,"* and when she didn't answer, he said in English, "Are you lost?"

That question made her lips lift in a smile. "Spiritually, I guess I am. Aren't we *all* lost? Are you Toshiro Ogama-san?"

"Yes."

"And are you accepting students? My name is Cynthia Tucker. You're translating one of my books for Hayakawa Shobo. I would have called first, but you don't have a phone listed. I'm in Japan for a month and a half, lecturing for the State Department and—well, since I'm *here,* and have a little unscheduled time, I was hoping to meet you, and discuss any problems you might have with American words in my book, and maybe get your help with my practice of meditation." Now she laughed, taking off her glasses. "Roshi, I think I need a *lot* of help."

"I . . . I'm not a teacher," said Toshiro.

"But you *are* the abbot of this beautiful temple, aren't you?"

"Yes . . ."

"Well, if it's all right, I'd love to stay a few days and—"

"Stay?" His voice slipped a scale.

"Yes, visit with you for a while and ask a few questions."
He was amused Tucker said this while standing under the
sign posted at every Zen temple and monastery, which read
LOOK UNDER YOUR FEET (for the answers), but this pilgrim
did not, of course, read Japanese. "I can make myself useful,"
she said. "And I won't be a bother. Maybe I can help you in
some way too."

As she spoke, and as he studied her more closely—her
flower-patterned blouse, sandals, and white slacks, how early
afternoon sunlight was like liquid copper in her hair, Toshiro
slowly realized that among the five books he was leisurely
translating for Hayakawa Shobo there *was* one by a Dr. Cynthia
Tucker, a Sanskrit scholar in the Asian Languages and Literature Department at the University of Washington. Her author's
bio and American newspaper interviews with her told him
she'd survived colon cancer, two divorces, had no children,
taught courses in Eastern philosophy, and described herself
whimsically as a Baptist-Buddhist. Her book, *The Power of a
Quiet Mind,* was a hefty six-hundred-page volume devoted to
interpreting the Dharma in terms that addressed the trials and
tribulations of black Americans. Toshiro was only two chapters
into his translation, but he'd found her work electrifying—even
culturally necessary. Her prose was incandescent, shimmering

with the Right Thought of all buddhas in the ten directions, but placed within a twenty-first-century black American context. Toshiro also found this ironic. In Japan, the old ways and old wisdom had become antique after World War II. The traditions of Soto and Rinzai Zen held little interest for this younger, business-minded generation of Japanese, who seemed quite satisfied pursuing the goods of the world and being salarymen. But the Americans? Since the 1960s, they had become passionate about the Dharma, even when they got it wrong, and he often suspected that much of the continuation of Asian spiritual traditions might fall to them, the *gaijin* of North America who had grown weary of materialism. As much as he valued his privacy at the temple, he saw how impolite it would be to turn this very distinguished visitor away. He wasn't happy about the prospect of having to be entertaining, but it couldn't be helped. If he didn't, her publisher—his boss—would not be pleased. Even so, he had always been awkward around people and felt afraid of this situation.

The young priest brought his palms together in the gesture of gratitude and veneration, called *gasshó,* and made a quick bow.

"Forgive me for not recognizing you at first. I think your book—and *you*—are wonderful, and you *can* help me with some of the words. But I don't think you should stay for too long. One day only. I don't see people often, and I'm not such a good teacher of the Buddhadharma. Really, I don't know *any*thing."

"Oh, that's hard to believe." The corners of her eyes crinkled as she smiled. "I've read that all beings are potential Buddhas. Anyone or anything can bring us to a sudden awakening—the timbre of a bell, an autumn rose, the extinguishing of a candle. Anything!"

Toshiro's eyes slipped out of focus when she said that. She really knew her stuff, and that made his heart give a very slight jump. How would she judge him if she knew the depths of his own failure? The priest invited the pilgrim inside, offering her a cup of rice wine and a plate of rice crackers. He showed her around the temple, the two of them sometimes walking out of step in their stocking feet and bumping each other as they conversed for half the afternoon about English grammar, with Tucker sometimes placing her hand gently on his shoulder, and peppering him with questions that made Toshiro's stomach chew itself—questions like What time do you get up? How often do you shave your head? Is your tongue on the roof of your mouth when you meditate? Do you eat meat, Roshi? Why are Zen priests in Japan allowed to get married, but not those in China? Toshiro noticed his palms were getting wet and wiped them on his shirt, but his arm still tingled with pleasure where she had touched him. He excused himself, saying he needed to work awhile on the stone garden he was creating. He repeated his apology, "I am the poorest of practitioners. You must ask someone else these questions. And not stay more than one night. People in the village will talk if a woman sleeps at the temple. And *don't* call me Roshi."

"I understand, I'll leave." Tucker put back her head and he could feel the smile on her face going frozen. "But Ogama-san, since I've come all this way across the Pacific Ocean, please give me something to do for the temple. I insist. I want to serve. I could make a donation, but college professors don't earn very much. I'd prefer to work. I could help you in your garden."

Not wanting that, and because the words left his mouth before his brain could catch them, he told Tucker that cleaning out one of the small storage rooms at the hinder part of the main hall, which contained items left over by the temple's last abbot fifty years ago, was a chore he'd been putting off since he moved into Anraku-ji. He gave her a broom, a mop, and a pail, then Toshiro, his stomach tied up in knots, hurried outside.

For the rest of the afternoon, he pottered about in the stone garden, but he was in fact hiding from her, and wondering what terrible karma had brought this always-questioning American to Anraku-ji. He was certain she would discover that, as a Zen priest, he was a living lie. He knew all the texts, all the traditional rituals, *every*thing about ceremonial training and temple management, but he had never to his knowledge directly experienced Nirvana. He feared he would never grasp *satori* during his lifetime. It would take a thousand rebirths for the doors of Dharma to crack open even a little for one as stalled on the Path by sorrow as Toshiro Ogama. In Japanese, there was a word for people like him: *Nise bozo*. It meant "imitation priest." And that was surely what Cynthia Tucker would judge him to be if he let her get too close, or linger too long on the temple grounds. If he was to save face, the only solution, as far as he could see, was to demand that she leave immediately.

At twilight, Toshiro tramped back to the main hall, intending to do just that. But what happened next, he had not expected. He found his visitor standing outside the storeroom, her hair lightly powdered with fine, gray dust, and heaped up around her in crates and cardboard boxes were treasures he never knew the temple contained. She had unearthed Buddhist prayers, *gatha*, written a hundred years before in delicate calligraphy on rice paper thin as theater scrim, and wall hangings elaborately painted on silk (these were called *kakemono*) that whispered of people who had passed through the temple long before he was born—past lives that were all the more precious because they were ephemeral, a flicker-flash of beauty against the backdrop of eternity. There were also large, pewter-gray tin canisters of film, a battered canvas screen, and a movie projector from the 1950s, which Tucker was cleaning with a moistened strip of cloth. When Toshiro stepped closer, she looked up, smiling, and said:

"When I was a little girl, my parents had a creaky, old projector kind of like this one. I think I can get it working, if you'd like to watch whatever is in those tin containers."

"*Yes*," said Toshiro, "I *would*." He picked up one of the canisters and read the yellowed label on top. "I can't believe this. These are like—how do you say?—home movies made here by my predecessor half a century ago."

Toshiro stepped aside as Tucker carried the screen and projector into the ceremony room. He plopped down on a cushion, watching her carefully thread film through sprocket wheels and test the shutter and lamp. Then she placed the blank screen, discolored by age, fifteen feet away next to the altar. She clicked off the lights. She threw the switch, and the old, obsolete projector began to whir. There was no sound, only the flicker of images on the tabula rasa of the screen, slowly at first, each frame discrete and separated from the others by spaces of white, as if the pictures were individual thoughts, complete in themselves, with no connection to the others—like *his* thoughts before he had his first cup of tea in the morning. Time felt suspended. But as the projector whirred on in the silent temple, the frames came faster, chasing each other, surging forward, creating a linear, continuous motion that brought a sensuously rich world to life before Toshiro's eyes. He realized he was watching a funeral in this very ceremony room, taped at Anraku-ji probably during the period of the Korean War. He felt displaced, not in space, but in time. On the screen, an elderly woman lay in state, surrounded by four grieving relatives, and long-stemmed white chrysanthemums. A thin blanket covered the old woman's shriveled body from her neck to her ankles. Someone had placed a small, white handkerchief over her face, and as a young man seated beside her, perhaps her eldest son, suddenly lifted the cloth and kissed her cold forehead, Toshiro felt his back shiver, the experience of ruin and abandonment that overcame him during his own parents' funeral welling up inside him once again. In spite of himself, he surrendered his personal anguish, his pain—the powerful energy of his emotions—over to the people at this funeral, and this transference thickened the screen so thoroughly that the young priest's nose clogged with mucus, his eyes burned with tears, but even as he sobbed uncontrollably, he knew himself to be locked in a cycle of emotion (his own) which these fleeting, black-and-white images borrowed, intensified, and gave back to him in a magic show produced by the mind, a dreamland spun from accelerated imagery. After a second, he realized this—yes, *this*—was what the sutras meant by *kamadhatu,* by the realm of illusion, by Samsara. By Prapanca. All at once, the ribbon of film in the projector broke, returning the screen to an expanse of emptiness completely untouched by the death and misery projected upon it. For these last few moments he had experienced not the world, but the workings of his own nervous system. And this was truly all he had *ever* known. He himself had been supplying the grief and satisfaction all along, from within. Yet his original mind, like the screen, remained Lotus flower pure and in a state of grace. At that moment, Toshiro Ogama understood. He knew. He saw clearly into his own self-nature, and forever lost the sense of twoness.

Outside, a breeze wuthered through yew trees and set chimes on the porch to ringing. Inside, the temple seemed to breathe, a gentle straining of wood on wood, then relaxation. Tucker clicked the lights on in the ceremony room. She saw tears streaming from Toshiro's eyes, and took a step toward him. "Ogama-san? Are you all right? I didn't know this would upset you so."

He rubbed his red eyes and stood up, self-emptied. "Neither did I. Thank you for working the projector."

She gave him a fast, curious look, and then moved to where her black, leather briefcase rested in a corner of the room. "I guess I'll be going now."

"Why?" said Toshiro. "In that film, I saw how once Anraku-ji was thriving with parishioners. There was a Sangha here of all sentient beings, and with no religious officials in sight. It should be that way again. Later this week I want to invite the villagers down the road to visit. Would you join my temple as its first member?"

The pilgrim did not speak, for words can be like a spider's-web. She simply bowed, pressing both brown palms together in *gasshó*—one palm symbolizing Samsara, the other Nirvana—in a gesture of unity that perfectly mirrored Toshiro's own.

Follow the Drinking Gourd

Think I heard the angels say,
Follow the drinkin' gourd.
Stars in the heaven gonna show you the way,
Follow the drinkin' gourd.

After escaping from slavery in Alabama, he went back willingly into the bleak, macabre world of slaves once again. Five years ago, in 1850, he'd fled the nightmare of bondage, with his wife, Adele, traveling by night from Mobile to Kentucky. It had been a hellish journey marked by weeks of hiding, disguises, last-minute escapes, and name changes. But after reaching Paducah, Kentucky, he kept moving and established himself in southern Illinois as a versatile craftsman based on the skills he'd learned as a bondsman. His name was Christian Fowler and, as Thoreau had written five years earlier about living in Walden, Fowler had developed during his thirty-five years as many "skills as fingers on the hand." He was a saddlemaker and carpenter, a barber and a cook. Of course, he was still a wanted man in Alabama, a fugitive with a $200 bounty on his head. There were padderolls and soulcatchers eager to collect that money if he showed himself anywhere near his old master's place. But why in the world would he do that? He had slipped away from bondage—the whippings, the sound of the daylight horn calling him to work—and built a decent life for himself from scratch. It was funny to him sometimes how slave owners could never understand why black people ran away. Their doctors even concocted a disease to explain this behavior—*drapetomania,* a sickness that supposedly made slaves flee their shackles and chains. Others just saw runaways as criminals—as people who had stolen *themselves* from their masters. At any rate, he was safe from all that in Illinois, and now Adele had given him two fine sons. Just the same, he *had* to go back to his borning ground, because never a night passed, as he and his family enjoyed the relative freedom of their new home, that he didn't have survivor's guilt and screamed himself awake when he saw in his dreams the faces of those family and friends he'd left behind when he cut dirt from the plantation of Captain William Boswell.

This would be his last trip. That was what he promised Adele. No more placing himself in danger after he guided to freedom her cousin Ida, a young woman around eighteen—perhaps two or three years younger—with chestnut-brown eyes, a mole beneath her ear like a grain of pepper, her hair arranged at the back in broad basket plaits, and her one-year-old baby, Sara. They'd been traveling light for weeks through backcountry that smelled mucilaginous and faintly sweet, through villages and tobacco fields, bringing only a little food, and Fowler carried his double-barreled shotgun, his bowie knife, and a canteen filled with old orchard to steady his nerves. As always, he followed that reliable beacon in the night—the Big Dipper stars, which were shaped, if you looked at them carefully, like a wooden gourd pointing to the pole star. "I've always been lucky," he'd told Adele when he left to rescue her cousin. "The North Star ain't never let me down. And God takes care of me."

But maybe not this time.

When they reached Mississippi, they'd covered a little more than half the distance to their destination, and he realized something was stalking them. Two men, soulcatchers, were a half a mile away, taking their time so as not to startle their prey, giving the runaways a little breathing room to relax and let down their guard before taking them by surprise. And he knew these two bounty hunters. Oh, yes, he even knew them by name. They were brothers, Caleb and Joshua Weems. He could smell them on the wind the way a rabbit did a hound. Now and then he could see their campfires. And they were good, those two, cagey and ruthless. The best man hunters in Alabama, who knew how runaways thought—it was rumored they had a little Negro blood, had at one time themselves been slaves—and they, with their savage tempers, had littered this landscape with slaves that resisted capture, wasting their lives like water. They'd done this ancient pas de deux together before. The eternal dance of death between the hunter and the hunted. They were in his dreams or—more precisely—in his exhausting, emotionally draining nightmares since he escaped from Captain Boswell.

Not far away, Fowler saw, off to his left, a lichened, twelve-stanchion barn, large, dark, and imposing, floating in the mist. He waisted Ida's short body with his free arm and guided her and the baby there over stumps and mudholes, miry places in thigh-high weeds, and brush-whipping tree branches. The entrance to the abandoned barn was boarded over. Fowler tore away the planks of plywood, pulling so hard the muscles in his neck bulged, and cutting his right hand on a rusty, square nail. Inside, the air felt tight, dead. Old farm equipment covered in gossamer-thin cobwebs was everywhere, as was an odor of musty hay and straw and old oats gone bad in their bins. The place was quiet as a temple, its silence floating hither and yon over old horse collars, sawhorses, scrap metal and lumber. He could hear Ida moan from a corner where she'd sat down in her heavy homemade, buckram skirt and was rocking the baby back and forth. She asked him if the men following them were going to take Sara and her back to Captain Boswell.

"No, honey." His voice was waxy, unused in hours, hoarse. "I won't let them take you back there."

Her eyes searched his face. "What about you?"

"We're going to wait here until them men are gone. But you have to keep that baby quiet. If she starts crying, they'll know right where we are."

"I think she's hungry," said Ida. "I can try to feed her."

She undid her blouse and turned her back to him. He was touched by her modesty and decided to step away as she breast-fed the baby, moving cautiously, his arms stretched wide. Night pressed against the window, but the hazy mist had distilled and he had a good view of the direction death or anything nocturnal might come in the darkness. Pieces of that same darkness were clinging to his congested mind. He could feel how tired he was of running, how light-headed from hunger. The gash where he'd cut his bloody hand throbbed. He needed rest. The temptation to just lie down in darkness, close his eyes, and let his mind sleep forever was overwhelming. But he remembered that new life, the home, he'd made in Illinois, the caring woman who he loved more than his own life. And their beautiful children, William and Zachary, who he loved beyond measure and prayed they would grow up free, knowing nothing of slavery in a place where you could go-as-you-pleased, a world so much better than the one he and Adele had somehow survived every day—even though, like a soldier, he still felt the trauma of once being enslaved. The damage, the fear of being recaptured, was still there like scar tissue. And a feeling that he didn't deserve freedom if everyone wasn't free, or maybe that being free was temporary, an illusion, and might be snatched away from him at any time. These thoughts, he knew, were mad. No one should suffer them. That was why he came back for Ida and baby Sara. But they would never know freedom and an end to the madness if a crying Sara gave away their location. For an instant—and it was an instant that made him hate himself—he remembered in the hindmost corner of his mind how Captain Boswell was oftentimes fond of quoting a poet named William Blake, whose words now trumpeted through his thoughts: *Sooner murder an infant in its cradle than nurse unacted desires.* That thought made his scalp crawl. If it came down to that, did he have the grit for silencing the baby—forever—to save Adele's cousin and himself? From the satchel slung over his shoulder, Fowler removed the canteen, then took a long pull, shuddering as the whiskey plunged down his throat pipe into his belly like a burning wire. Strong drink erased the image of infanticide in William Blake's poem from his mind. Drink dulled the pain in his hand and made veins stand out on his temples. He, the hunted, lumbered back toward Ida, feeling the darkness like a blind man, fighting his terrible exhaustion, found with a painful crack the edge of a mule's harness with his shin, suppressed the urge to swear, and kept his eyes to the left of her, because she was still trying to nurse a mewling baby who might at any moment let fly with a cry that would condemn them both again to beatings and chattel bondage.

"You gotta keep her quiet, okay?"

"I'm tryin'." Her voice was shaky. "But she's teething, and I think she caught her death-a-cold. You know, from all the nights we had to sleep on the ground when the weather was wet. Here, feel her forehead."

She lifted the baby toward him. Sara was burning up beneath his fingers. He took the canteen from his satchel and handed it to Ida. "Spread some of this on her gums. That might he'p to quiet her some." Then he said, looking into her eyes, "There's something else—something really important—I need for you to do for me. You remember that song I taught you? I want you to sing it for me. Real soft. Just whisper the words to me."

"Why?"

"Don't question me." He drew his mouth down, and looked hard at her. "I have my reasons." Then he cut the sudden harshness in his voice by half when he saw how Ida's face, like those of everyone who lived enslaved, always relaxed into a beautiful yet fragile mask of sadness. "That song will save your life," he said. "Please, just sing it."

And so she did, her voice soft-breathing, gently singsong, so beautiful a contralto, controlled and clear, that it lifted him out of himself, reminding him of how his wife often sang as she worked, and he almost forgot the life-or-death urgency behind his need to make sure she got every word right. "Sing that last part again for me, all right?"

"All right." She lifted her head. "The river bank will make a mighty good road / The dead trees show you the way / The river ends between two hills / There's another on the other side / Follow the drinkin' gourd where the great river meets the little river."

"Good. Very good."

Just as he took a little heart at this, as something in him relaxed, as he started to think with a smile of getting back home, there came from baby Sara a cascade of chest-shattering screams that filled the barn, filled the night outside, and filled Fowler's ears like explosions. It felt to him as if she cried for an eternity, and he stared—just stared—helplessly at the child as Ida tried to quiet her, unbuttoning her blouse again, revealing her small, pear-shaped, brown-nippled breasts—this time Fowler didn't look away. But he was coiled up inside, his teeth grating, silently trying to will the child into silence, thinking, *Be quiet, be still,* noticing only now that his right hand had picked up a chump of wood from the floor to silence her squall. Was he about to kill the child? He couldn't tell. But Ida finally got the baby to suck. The wide-ribbed barn was quiet again. He let the wood slip from his hand.

He stepped back to the window, his knees feathery, and sat there like a statue with his head tipped and shoulders crushed down for a long, long time, emptied of hope. Emptied of all thoughts of himself. Everything was simple now. Had the hunters heard those high-pitched, earsplitting screams? He was certain-sure they had. There was no way to repair what the baby had done, no more than he could unring a bell. Like as not, the slave catchers were on their way. He was dead already. And he knew what he had to do. What any righteous, right-thinking person in this situation would do. It was time to dance again with devils. After gathering himself together, he opened his satchel. Silently, he removed

68

two shells. Silently, he carefully examined his shotgun, snapping both triggers and checking the firing pin before loading both barrels and closing the breech. And silently, he waited, there at the window, where the moon was an hour higher since he'd last looked at the sky, feeling peace, a kind of gallows serenity he could not describe, as if suddenly he could accept and welcome whatever came, that he had no fear and was equal to any task, no matter how difficult or distasteful it might be. He grasped the shotgun by its carved pistol grip, the stock placed under his arm against his body, the butt pushed into his armpit. As he pressed the barrels more firmly against his left leg, his thoughts lapsed to a line from John 15: *Greater love hath no man . . .* but the words broke off when he heard away in the night the breathing of horses. He could feel his face stretch at the sound, then sure enough, he caught a glimpse of two travel-stained, spectral shapes materializing out of the mist. Fowler shot a glance toward Ida, one finger pressed to his lips. When the men dismounted from horses with rags tied to their hooves—a gray Medley and the other an Appaloosa—he could see, in a splash of silver moonlight, Caleb Weems, husky, hairy-necked, ponderous but quick as a trout, his head rammed forward, craning his neck to cock a look toward the barn door, and right behind Caleb was his toad-like, bandy-legged, jug-eared older brother, Joshua, with hair like moldy hay, carrying an owlhead pistol, half of him covered by a horseman's cloak white from road dust, both of them advancing toward the barn like wolves. Ida was standing now, holding her daughter on her hip. Over his shoulder, he flung a whisper to her, *No matter what comes of me, no matter what you see next, follow the North Star.*

Then he waited, his teeth set, bone against bone, as Joshua nosily blew his nose in his hand and in a roosterish voice told Caleb to check the barn. Waited, being now the trapper and the trapped, as the barn door creaked on its hinges. Now it opened, and Fowler made a hissing in-take of breath. It opened, he saw Joshua step inside, and the hunted blew the hunter to Kingdom Come. He bolted outside, clambered over Joshua's shattered body, and, his chest pounding, rammed the stock of his shotgun against the side of Caleb's head. He ran south, swift as a deer. Ran so hard he felt he was nothing but legs and burning lungs.

After a moment, his running slowed to a few steps and he stopped, facing round, pausing to make sure an enraged Caleb, bent on revenge for his brother's death and not thinking clearly, was pursuing him. When he saw the hunter closing the distance, he—the hunted—smiled bleakly. If something happened to him, if he could not outrun or outwit Caleb, then his argument was that he had known happiness and freedom before—let that do—and Ida and her baby would know it now, because "Follow the Drinkin' Gourd" was much more than a song. It was a black American charm with back-and-hidden instructions in every stanza. A coded message only Negroes on the run could know. A detailed map for someone to follow to freedom. The first river was the Tombigbee, which would take them to Mobile Bay. The two hills were Woodall Mountain and a smaller one at the highest point in Mississippi. Earlier, he'd marked the dead trees with charcoal as a sign. The ribbon of river on the other side was the Tennessee. Its left-hand side would take them to the Ohio River and to Paducah, Kentucky, where his wife, Adele, would be waiting. Yes, he thought, as he started to run again, so fast his feet seemed scarcely to touch the ground, yes, they would be fine. And that meant, one way or another, he would be fine, too.

Idols of the Cave

S *tate my name for the record?*
All right. Wahab Khan.

Do I understand why I'm on trial? Do I understand the seriousness of the charges against me?

Yes, sir, I do. But sometimes I wonder if it really happened, or if someone told me a story about it.

You're on trial facing a court-martial, years in prison, and maybe execution. It began when the villagers in Afghanistan's Bamiyan valley told the government that the Taliban had returned. They forced the villagers out of the caves where they had been living. There were three thousand honeycombing caves that had been hacked out of sandstone two millennia ago by Buddhist monks who believed in the inescapable interconnectedness and non-duality of all things. They ran alongside holes where two huge statues of the Buddha used to stand in the dun-colored sandstone Bamiyan cliffs before the Taliban blasted them with tank fire and dynamite. The governor of Bamiyan said those caves were one of his country's cultural treasures. "We have caves," he said, "that even the Devil doesn't know about." So to rid the area of insurgents, you couldn't use your standard tactic of dropping five thousand pounds of bunker-buster bombs to seal entrances and ventilation shafts. Leave it to the military to never make things easy. You're here on trial because you and your platoon had to clear those ancient caves of insurgents, room by room.

Was Afghanistan hard on me? Are you kidding? Every day was hell. It was such a tragedy we couldn't bring ourselves to say our drawdown was a retreat because the U.S. military never retreats. So we called it a tactical retrograde.

The worst part of your tour wasn't the camel spiders and scorpions you found in your clothes and boots, or getting G.I. (gastrointestinal) that kept you shitting brown soup all day, or the nasty-tasting hydration tablets, or being your team's combat medic, or the powdery moon dust that covered everything in southern Afghanistan. No, the worst part was the constant fatigue. And the worst part of the fatigue wasn't it being physical but in your case psychological, because as a Muslim American soldier, you always had to prove yourself to narrow-minded people like your commanding officer, Major Billy Joe Tyler, a Christian countryboy from Mississippi, a fierce defender of his faith who was always on your case, pulling your chain, because he thought you were a candy ass since you went to college, majoring in Middle Eastern classics, and because, as he once put it, "My God is bigger than your god. My tribe is stronger than yours. I mean, why are you even *here*, Wahab? You're going to kill us the first chance you get, aren't you? So you can get your seventy-two virgins in heaven, right?"

Major Tyler was blond, thirty-five years old, with a sweaty voice, squint lines around his seven-mile stare, and a classic weight lifter's body—short forearms and legs, a broad chest, with maybe eight pounds of pure muscle on his upper body, which probably meant he'd be dead by forty from the strain on his heart. You tried to keep your distance from him, because he had so many tattoos stamped on his body they made your eyes swim—one tat between his shoulder blades was a saying by General James Mattis: *Be polite, be professional, but have a plan to kill everybody you meet.* Needless to say, Major Tyler fell a little short on the politeness part. Added to which, and most of all, he was deliberately dirt-ignorant about other countries and people of a different confession. Whenever you took a moment to step away from the barracks and offer morning prayers, he started singing "What a Friend We Have in Jesus" as soon as you came back into the room. You guess he sensed how much you disliked and feared him, because he was always testing you with little, casual microaggressions and drive-by put-downs. Testing your loyalty and patriotism, as he put it. Most of the time he called you by any name but your own.

What's that? Did I hate Major Tyler? No, I wouldn't say that. I guess we both were just trapped in the cages of our different cultures.

75

You remember one day when everyone in your section of the platoon was shoveling a few hundred sandbags, regular Joes and officers in their shorts and flip-flops, no rank visible, because fortifying your defenses was everyone's job. It was hot work, and every so often Tyler stopped, dripping sweat, looking at you with a smirk, and finally said, "Abdul, I read that if something isn't in the *Qur'an,* you Muslims believe it's unimportant and it just has to go like the way T-man blowed up those Buddha statues. But if it *is* in the *Qur'an,* then you don't need it so it *still* just has to go. Do you practice that? *My* people, my tribe wouldn't do that. That's why we're at war. A holy war, like the Crusades."

You told him, quietly, that you believed in appreciating and preserving valuable things from other cultures. That was an Islamic tradition, one violated by the Taliban and the butchers in Daesh who preached a mad doctrine of error to the world. Under your breath, you prayed for Allah to keep you safe and show this kafir and the others that you were just as American as they were—a second-generation citizen after your parents came from Turkey, but these days nobody would suspect that given the way your dad, a doctor, and your brother, Raheel, a computer technician, were always detained at airports, and the way kids in middle school teased your sister, Shawna, by tearing off her head scarf. Being Muslim in 2017 was, you decided, a bit like how black people could never move carelessly in a country like ours, how you always had to hold yourself to a higher standard, how you were always involved with the real meaning of *jihad*, which is an "inner struggle," a critical self-examination aimed at the goal of achieving peace. You never had the luxury of making mistakes. Major Tyler, sensing this about you, that you often were torn between deciding if something was *halal* (permissible) or *haram* (prohibited) by your faith, was always trying to trip you up.

When you arrived at the caves, he said, "Abdul, I don't think I'd trust you in a crunch, but since you act like you think you're better'n everybody else, and talk like a syllabus, why don't *you* take point?"

As ordered, you took lead, moving slowly away from the abandoned village in the valley in scorching, 90-degree July heat, sweat streaming inside your uniform. You could hear a stray dog barking its brains out, every exhalation a yelp, but you tried not to let it distract you. You moved slowly, hunched forward, because of all that gear you, as a combat medic, had to wear—helmet, a submachine gun and shotgun for close-quarters combat, and eighty pounds of equipment and medicine in your rucksack. And since this was a combat mission to clear out those caves, you had a respirator, earplugs, and night-vision goggles.

You climbed easily enough up to the entrance to one of the circular caves fifteen meters wide by fifteen meters long, and signaled for the others to follow. Twenty soldiers were in your Special Forces urban warfare unit. Major Tyler and Jimmy Doyle, a plucky kid with mouse-like eyes and a flat, pale face, shook out, running ahead of the others. Entering the cave cautiously, you could see the Taliban had been there, and might be there still. They'd left ammunition, supplies, and propaganda. You stepped closer to examine the munitions, but that's when you heard a salvo of machine-gun fire from what your intel told you was *supposed* to be an abandoned village. Intel? That was a joke. The guesstimates and maps the higher-ups gave you were called the Comics or the Funny Pages by everyone in your company. Suddenly that flawed intel put you in a firefight, the others caught in a crossfire, and the mission turned into a damned soup sandwich. Tyler and Doyle scrambled into the cave seconds before a rocket-propelled grenade hit the entrance and knocked you to your knees. Your earplugs had been in the open position when you approached the caves so you could distinguish between hostile acts and natural sounds in the environment. But that explosion passed right through the open position of your plugs. All of a sudden, you were deaf, straining to hear Major Tyler shouting like someone underwater as he told Jimmy Doyle, dazed by the blast, not to keep backing into the cave, which was what he was doing, and that's when he stepped on the pressure sensor of a buried IED that blew up the ground and sent you plummeting ten feet into a subterranean chamber.

Excuse me, what did you say? What did we find in the chamber? What was hidden there? I'll get to that in a moment, sir.

When you hit bottom, you were so dazed for a few seconds your eyes were swimming, and you didn't move until you heard a groan angle across the air from Major Tyler. You were experiencing pain yourself—skin was torn away from your ribs—and you could taste blood in your mouth. You'd both come crashing down in darkness hot, rubbery, through the ceiling of a sealed chamber onto rows of clay water jugs that broke open when you landed on them, spilling their contents—Buddhist scrolls written on birch bark in some pots and works in Arabic. Your first thought was that they'd cushioned your fall. Your second thought was that if you were injured, this was a blessing because it would be the end of your tour, your ticket home.

And it would have been except for what happened next.

You heard the major moan again. You found your tactical flashlight, flicked it on, and when its seven hundred lumens lit up the cave, you saw him lying a few feet away from Doyle, whose head was smashed open like a melon. Dark blood was guttering from a raw, ugly gash in the major's side, caused by shrapnel. You moved toward him, aching in every fiber, your knees feathery, tore away only enough of his clothing to expose the wound, then applied direct pressure with your hands to keep him from bleeding out. You checked him for additional wounds. In your backpack, you found hemostatic dressings (HemCon) and pressed it against his wound for two minutes to stop the hemorrhaging. He looked dazed and frightened and confused, but he was conscious and praying to *his* god when it was *you* giving him oral antibiotics from your combat pill pack.

You said, "How're we doin'?"

Tyler began another moan, but cut it off, releasing instead a cough. "You tell me. Is this place gonna be my coffin?"

"I don't think so," you said. "Be still. We're just having a bad day."

He made a feeble smile. "You think?" Then his eyes bent up to meet yours. "Wahab, I guess I was wrong about you. I apologize. In your religion, in mine, we both need something to struggle against."

You didn't answer, but that, of course, was an answer. After inspecting his dressing again, you said, "We'll be okay. They're coming for us. There has to be a dustoff inbound right now for rescue. All we have to do is just wait here—wherever *here* is."

"Don't take me to an Afghan hospital. I'll die waitin' to be treated. I want American, you understand?"

You told him you did.

"And where the hell are we?"

"I think we're in what used to be an ancient library," you said. "The IED unsealed it. Even the Taliban probably didn't know it was here."

He gave a slight headshake. "What's all this stuff on the floor?"

You were wondering the same thing yourself, and swung your flashlight's beam away from Tyler and around a chamber that looked like a holy ruin. Once upon a time, two thousand monks meditated in these caves. Time had accumulated in the air and thousand-year-old walls covered with the oldest oil paintings in the world—scenes from Buddhist mythology, left there by monks and travelers on the Silk Road. Above you, there were clusters of skittish bats and, at your feet, their droppings—guano—turned white by time, crumbly, frail as ash. The air felt thick enough to tear with your nails like tissue. All around you on the rocky floor, in a room of tombed wonders and rarities, were fragments of clay pots, the ancient writings they contained, and artifacts from Egypt, India, Persia, and China, for Bamiyan in its Hinayana Golden Age was at the crossroads of the world. You lifted from the raff of rubble a sheath of time-discolored treatises preserved over the centuries by the dry, shady condition of the cave, and you looked and saw . . .

Saw what no one had ever seen in their wildest dreams.

"Major," you whispered, "these pots are full of Arab manuscripts."

"So?" he said. "This is fuckin' Afghanistan, ain't it?"

With all the dust in the air, you swallowed to wet the inside of your mouth. "Sir, *this* stack of pages—right *here*—with commentary by the great Arab scholar Avicenna, is Aristotle's *Physics,* his *Metaphysics,* his *De Anima,* his *Poetics,* and"—you held your breath—"his treatise on comedy. This is like finding the Dead Sea Scrolls."

Tyler was trying to understand the importance of what you were saying, but having a hard time. "You said comedy. What is it? A joke book?"

You wiped away dust and cobwebs from the wafer-thin pages, reading the text with a slow finger. "Well, yes. I think I see a joke here."

"Tell it to me."

"Okay . . . Two cannibals are eating a clown. One stops and says to the other, 'Does this taste funny to you?' "

The major laughed, and that made him clutch his side and groan again. But laughter in a situation like this was good. "Tell me another one."

"Uh, okay. Here's one. Never bet on a racehorse named Zeno."* Tyler's eyebrows drew inward with thought. He scratched his neck. "I don't get that one."

But then you were so excited you started talking out loud more to yourself than him as you thumbed through Aristotle's lost treatise, remembering that *he,* Aristotle, used to stutter, hated children, and was never quite accepted by the Athenians because he was an outsider from Macedonia. All his works and even the skill of reading were lost during the catastrophic European Dark Ages, but when Muslims conquered Syria they discovered there a treasure trove of Greek culture that came from the earlier conquests of Alexander the Great, a student of Aristotle, and these works they preserved (as you would preserve this work on comedy) when they swept across North Africa into Spain, thus reintroducing arts and sciences to European Christendom, giving the West back Aristotle, the inventor of formal logic, general science, and an understanding of marine biology that was not improved

* Both jokes for Aristotle's treatise on comedy were provided by literary scholar John Whalen-Bridge of the National University of Singapore.

on until the nineteenth century. And all that set the stage for the fifteenth-century information explosion that we called the Renaissance.

What's that? Did the major accept what I was saying? Did he understand this history? Well, I thought so . . .

Indeed, he had been quietly listening to you, his lips tightly pressed together, his eyes crimped and thoughtful. "So," he said, "this pagan joke book is going to make Christians see themselves *in* Muslims? As *being* Muslims? Like we're mirrors of each other? Joined at the hip or something like that?"

"We *are* forever joined," you said. "Ninety-five percent of what is in Christianity is in Islam. The word *muslim* means 'one who does the will of God,' and Jews and Christians once called themselves that. Maybe Aristotle's treatise will be seen as yet another gift from the Arab world that made Western civilization possible. That the East-West division is false."

After a second, Tyler gave a headshake. "Good. Maybe now we'll finally have some peace. Look, I'm okay. You saved my life. You ought to rest a little yourself now. We'll be medevaced out of here soon . . ."

You *were* exhausted. Your thoughts were growing cloudy. Leaning back against a wall, pressing the precious treatise tight against your chest, you let your eyelids lower, drifting off into a sleep that felt more like stupor than rest, descending through an intricate gallery of dovetailing dreams as delicate as dioramas, where you saw the Western world set on fire by your discovery, which was priceless, though you would, of

course, set a hefty price on it and become incredibly rich.
Never mind that the treatise was legally the property of the
people of Afghanistan, you saw yourself publishing articles
in proper journals, explaining on TV to the vast majority of
monocultural Americans, who knew nothing about Aristotle,
let alone Islam, that he left us so little in the *Poetics* about comedy, saying only that it concerned men worse than ourselves,
though they were not necessarily evil, only ridiculous, while
tragedy depicted men better than ourselves, yet *this* discovery
filled in all the details of what more one of the greatest minds
in history had to say on this subject. But then in the depths
of your dream the document disintegrated, slipping through
your fingers like sand, and you lumbered awake, coughing
from smoke. The treatise was gone. A few feet away, Tyler
was stoking the embers of a small fire, his eyes evasive, but
on his lips a little grin of triumph quivered round his mouth.
Without asking, you knew by the knotting of your belly, by
the racing of your heart, what he'd done and why. Of course,
you thought, this is how it always ends. How it has to end.
Nothing lasts forever.

Here in a cave carved out of stone by Buddhist monks
who within its walls sang prayers of how no distinction
existed between I and thou and that everything was a part
of everything else, here in a war zone that had defeated the
Russians, then the Americans, here you slowly became aware
that you'd picked up your shotgun. You listened only to the
blood pulsing in your ears as you inspected two shells, then

loaded both barrels, feeling only a weak rage as you fell deeper into relativity, closed the breech, and in those few, fibrous seconds cocked both triggers. The ricocheting sound of the blast sent bats skirring and screaking throughout the chamber like a swarm of bees.

Yes, that's all I remember, sir. I was passed out when the rescue team got to us. What's that? Do I think I'm guilty? Yeah, I do. We all are. Guilty as hell. When it comes down to thinking we're better than someone else, I don't think any of us are clean. But the one thing I can't figure out. You know what that is? I'm sure Aristotle would say what we experienced in that cave was a calamity. But what I'm still trying to understand is if he would say all of this was a comedy or a tragedy. Or maybe both.

Occupying Arthur Whitfield

O n a Sunday night in early October, just moments after
I dropped off a fare at the Lucid jazz lounge in the
University District, I got the call from dispatch to pick up
my last passenger.

"Antwon," said Denise, the dispatcher, through her radio,
"you want this one? I could give it to Akeem, but he's in West
Seattle. This place is only ten minutes away from where you
are. And you've still got forty minutes on your shift."

"I'll take it," I said. "Then I'm going home. Who am I
picking up?"

"He says his name is Arthur Whitfield. He's at 241 East
Interlaken Boulevard, and he needs to get to Sea-Tac for a
red-eye flight at two A.M."

"No problem," I said. "I'll get him there. You think he's
good for a decent tip? I need that green."

"Well, you never know. This guy might be loaded. So be
nice to him."

The address Denise gave me was in a neighborhood where

some homes were selling for between $700,000 and $900,000. For some reason I thought I recognized the pickup's name. There was something familiar about it, but I couldn't quite put my finger on what that was. On the backseat of my cab, there was a copy of *The Seattle Times* left there by a fare I'd taken earlier to Lake City. I only went as far as high school, but I did a year of community college before my money ran out, and I still love to read, so whenever somebody leaves a magazine or a book on the backseat I save it so I can have something to look at during my lunch break. I put the cab in neutral, clicked on the ceiling light, and reached for the paper. The front page, above the crease, was filled with a story about the Occupy Seattle protesters, who had taken over Westlake Park, speaking truth to power. Even though I hadn't made it to that demonstration, everything happening there hit pretty close to home for me.

When I say "close to home," I mean that literally. A place of my own, even my own apartment, was one of those things, like finishing college, that I knew I'd never be able to afford after the meltdown in America that threw us all back to the way my grandparents talked about the Great Depression. At twenty-two, I was living with my Baptist mother in her tiny house that shook all day long from trucks that pounded through the Central District, in the same cramped cubbyhole of a bedroom I had when I was a child, and she didn't even own that place. The bank did, so my mom still had decades to go before her mortgage was paid. After the mild stroke she had a year ago (with no health insurance to cover it), I don't know where she finds the strength to keep making a way out of no way for both of us. For seeing windows where I saw walls. But I guess black folks have been doing that for hundreds of years. Still, I hate it when I see her bringing home jars of Department of Agriculture peanut butter. The very sight of that welfare food made me feel ashamed. It killed my appetite. Everything about our hardscrabble lives of daily sacrifice made me feel ashamed and second-rate. She was starting to look like a husk of the woman she'd been before the Great Recession. She looked used up and worn out, and I kept wondering what the hell *was* wealth? Why did a few people have so much and all the rest, nothing? Sometimes I'd stand in the hallway between the living room and the kitchen with its buckled linoleum floor, looking critically at everything we owned—the dining room table, the sofa and chair, and the cheap reproductions of paintings on the walls. All of it was used, secondhand, scarred, falling apart, some of it from the Salvation Army and yard sales. In other words, we didn't have *any*thing of value. All I could do was shake my head and wonder if we'd ever be able to live large like that one percent the Occupy Seattle people were protesting.

So there I was, just another poor, young black man driving a beat-up jitney, with no prospects, and pissed off because just thinking about all this, the way 99 percent of us had to struggle, how Social Security probably wouldn't exist when I needed it, made me so mad sometimes my hands started to shake, and I'd feel myself heating up with hatred for rich people, so I turned away from that first section of the paper, looking for the news story I thought I remembered seeing about Whitfield.

It was there, just like I thought, and where I should have looked in the first place. The business section. The story wasn't long. It was about three people Microsoft was hiring for its advanced research group. There were photos of the three, that fella Whitfield among them. He was one of those cutting-edge technorati with deep pockets. You know the kind I mean. The ones who really *do* believe they should be running the world. Have you ever taken a hard look at the logo for Apple? There's a *bite* taken out of its right side, like the one Eve gave to Adam, the original sin that got us all kicked out of paradise. The story said that six years ago Microsoft bought a company Whitfield created on the East Coast. Like the other two techies, he was in transit, moving his life and belongings from Beantown to the Northwest. Specifically, to Interlaken.

So fifteen minutes after I talked with dispatch, there I was, coasting slowly along a tree-lined street, looking for his address. I saw it, a two-story Tudor on a slope—a beautiful house, probably built in the 1920s, and I'm guessing it had a nice view of Mount Baker. Pulling up in front of his place, I saw a middle-aged man, maybe fifty years old (maybe sixty) fumbling with the lock on his front door—he looked pretty hammered—then he suddenly stooped down, almost falling, and did something to the doormat. When I tapped my horn, he almost jumped out of his expensive-looking, custom-made black suit, and looked round at my jitney in surprise. I stepped out of the cab and had the trunk open by the time he reached the curb with his brown leather suitcase, which I took from him, saying, "How you doing this evening, Mr. Whitfield?"

"I've been worse," he replied.

I found that hard to believe, and for a second I wondered if this tetchy, little man was channeling Steve Jobs. His movements were quick, impatient, like he had half a hundred duties barnacled to his life, like he was somebody used to barking out orders and having them obeyed. His green eyes, the shade of money, never made contact with mine, as if he didn't see me as real, or worth either his time or his attention. Dispatch had told me to be nice, so I tried my best. I held out my hand for a grip and grin, but he ignored it. I scurried around the side of the cab and opened the rear door for him to climb inside. He didn't seem to know how to say thank you.

Back behind the wheel, clicking on the ceiling light, I tried to catch a glimpse of his face in my rearview mirror. He had a great head of vanilla hair like Newt Gingrich, thick glasses, and a thin voice, and there was a strange, ugly scar on his forehead. I could see GOP in every grain of this guy. And whatever he'd been drinking—bourbon maybe—perfumed the inside of my cab with an odor so strong it made me cough.

In a fast, high-pitched voice that was anything but soothing, he said, "Take me to Sea-Tac."

"Yes, *sir*," I said. "Right away."

I turned off the light, turned on the meter and station 98.9 so I could hear some soft jazz, and headed southeast toward Twenty-Fourth Avenue East. From there I got onto Montlake Boulevard, made my way to 520 West, and after ten minutes the tires on my cab were humming along Interstate 5. To pass the time, I said, "You flying domestic or international?"

"Domestic. Delta." I could hear him sigh. "I'm going to Boston."

I nodded. "Business or pleasure?"

Whitfield left a silence. He had the strange habit of rubbing his knees when he talked. Then, almost as if I wasn't there, he said, "Neither. I may be gone for a week. I have to be in court . . . to testify."

I figured I'd better leave *that* alone. Maybe he was being sued for patent infringement or something. Cautiously, I said, "I guess your family will miss you while you're gone."

"They're in Boston," he said. "I have to bring them here. Listen, Antwon, is that what you call yourself?" He pitched himself forward, one hand on the back of my seat, squinting over his glasses at the photo identification of me in my dreadlocks on the dashboard, sounding the two syllables of my first name like he couldn't stand their taste on his tongue. "I don't feel like talking. Is that okay with you?"

"Sure."

"And turn off the radio. I don't want to hear music."

I did as he told me.

We rode for another fifteen minutes in total silence. I guess he felt servants should be seen and not heard. I could smell whiskey on him like a sickness so I rolled down my window an inch or two. And all that time, as I lane-changed toward the exit for Sea-Tac, my mind was working overtime. He was a rich asshole. Both a nerd and a turd. There was no doubt about that. But he'd just made the enormous mistake of telling me that he'd be gone for a week, and that his family wasn't in that big old, expensive house. This was low-hanging fruit. In other words, it was a ripe opportunity for a little redistribution of wealth. And what was wrong with that? You could see this dude had more of life's good things than he needed, and maybe even deserved. I hadn't made it over to Occupy Seattle, but here was my chance to do my part for the oppressed— namely, myself—by Occupying Whitfield. That idea had me smiling to myself when I stopped in front of Delta, then pulled his suitcase from the trunk. I didn't even mind when this prick handed me his pocketful of change for a tip, then hurried inside. What he gave me came to all of one dollar and forty-seven cents. I leaned back against my cab for moment, picking out the pennies, flicking each one into the street on top of a crunched-up condom. Then I drove right over them, and kept the front windows in my cab wide open to clear out his smell until I was two blocks from his house in Interlaken, and that's where I parked.

I keep a flashlight in my glove compartment. I took it with me when I walked up the street as wind rushed through the plumage of trees overhead. I sprinted up the steps to his front door, then lifted the black, rubber doormat to see why he'd been fooling with it. Underneath, as I expected, I saw an envelope, and inside that there was a letter with instructions for his cleaning lady—a woman probably as poor as my mother— and a front door key. I let myself in, holding my breath, feeling for just a second as if I was slipping myself into Whitfield's soul. I let the door click shut, relieved that I didn't hear one of those ADT alarms going off, but now I found myself standing in total darkness, my heart tightening in my chest, and sweat was trickling down the back of my T-shirt. With two fingers I wiped perspiration off my forehead and let the flashlight beam guide me along hardwood floors on the first level from room to room, and what I saw humbled me.

Compared to my mother's house, this place seemed palatial. There was a big fireplace, four bathrooms, and a spacious Viking kitchen where moonlight streamed through the windows. I almost wanted to hang my head, feeling that places like this would always be foreign to me. But what struck me as strange was that there wasn't much furniture. And while one bathroom cabinet was loaded with Zoloft, Paxil, and Risperdal, the kitchen cupboard was bare. The refrigerator was empty except for a few cans of Budweiser—I cracked one open—a loaf of Sara Lee bread, and bricks of cheddar and Swiss cheese.

Upstairs there was only one bed with the sheets and blankets all tangled together. I'm guessing Whitfield had been living here for only a couple of weeks, not even long enough to get a security system installed, and he was probably planning on buying furniture after he relocated his family. There was a framed picture of them on a nightstand in the bedroom. They were all standing on a sailboat, smiling at the camera. On the far right was Whitfield, his arm around a teenage girl. Brown freckles were sprinkled across her nose, she was wearing braces, and had her arm wrapped around a woman with a gentle smile and long brown hair who was so pretty I had to stare at her for a few seconds. Together like that, they looked like the perfect, privileged WASP family. I threw their photo on the bed, and kept looking in vain in the second-, then first-floor rooms for something I could liberate.

Finally, I found my way down into the basement. On one side there was a utility room with a washing machine and dryer, on the other I saw a room that had been converted into an office, or a den. In there were two cardboard cartons shipped UPS to this house from an address in Boston. On the side of each carton there was a name written in black Magic Marker: KATHERINE ASHLEY.

I pried open the carton with KATHERINE written on the side first, and I hit the jackpot. I couldn't believe what I was looking at, all that was right there just for the taking. Several wooden hand-tooled boxes were filled with expensive jewelry, and I realized how he must really feel this woman, Katherine, his wife, was all the good there was in the world. He'd showered her with diamonds and gold trinkets as if she was Her Majesty Queen Elizabeth II. In that one carton, there were glittering necklaces, gold rings, broaches, articles of clothing from French fashion houses, bracelets, and pelf I could pawn for thousands of dollars. I started cramming everything I could into the pockets of my cargo pants, and even inside my shirt, but then something in balled-up newspaper used at the bottom of the carton to cushion its contents caught my eye. On one page there was a family photo of the Whitfields identical to the one framed in the upstairs bedroom. Above that were mug shots of three men, all brothers with the last name Osborn.

My hands started to tremble. My eyes panned down through a few paragraphs, and I come to find out that four months ago, right after Whitfield was in the news because he made a killing when he sold his company, the brothers Osborn targeted his family for a home invasion—just like *I* was doing. They broke in wearing bandannas over their faces. One of them hit Arthur Whitfield in the face with a large cast-iron skillet he found in the family's kitchen. They bound father, mother, and daughter with duct tape. Two of them repeatedly raped Katherine and Ashley while the third ransacked the house for cash and jewelry. Then, to destroy any DNA evidence, they set the house on fire. Only Arthur survived this gasoline grave, but probably wished he hadn't. All three brothers were caught. The remains of his wife and daughter, who died from smoke inhalation, were cremated. He was bringing them here, I realized, in two urns. The trial for the first of the Osborn brothers was set to begin tomorrow.

The beer I'd been drinking from the fridge backwashed in my throat. I felt sick. I felt, in fact, that I *had* stepped inside his soul and found it to be ravaged. In a single night *every-thing* he loved and worked for had been taken away in a hard lesson that whoever we are, however rich, there was nothing we could ever hang onto. Slowly, I emptied my pockets. I put back what I'd taken, slipped out the back door, and as quickly as I could put distance between myself and the house of the most impoverished passenger I'd ever had in my cab.

When I got behind the wheel, I just sat for a spell, thinking about him. And then about my mother. I didn't hate him anymore. I pitied him. Ain't that a bitch? A po' colored man like me pitying *him*? All of a sudden I felt something in my cargo pants pressing against the seat. I reached into one of the side pockets, and what I pulled out was a diamond bracelet I'd forgotten to put back. I felt an impulse to sneak again into the house on Interlaken Boulevard, returning it to where it belonged. But the woman for whom it was intended was gone. Instead, I cranked the key in the car's ignition, and I pointed its hood in the direction of the Central District. God forgive me if what I did was wrong, but I figured that bracelet belonged on the arm of my hardworking mom.

Welcome to Wedgwood

A new Rasmussen Reports survey finds that 69 percent of
Americans think their fellow countrymen are becoming
more rude and less civilized. Men are much more likely
than women to have confronted someone over their rude
behavior, though more women than men think sales and
service personnel are more rude than they were a decade
ago. Adults over age fifty are more likely than their younger
counterparts to think it is rude for someone sitting next to
them in public to talk on their cell phone.

> —Associated Press news item

I have learned silence from the talkative, toleration from
the intolerant, and kindness from the unkind; yet, strange
I am ungrateful to those teachers.

> —Kahlil Gibran

The trouble started on a late afternoon in September.
It was around six P.M., and I was sitting under one of
the trees in my backyard, watching a brace of pigeons splash

wildly around in our stone birdbath, beneath which a stone head of the Buddha rose up from the grass. My dog, Nova, a West Highland white terrier, rested peacefully nearby. I've always loved this hour of the day, when the spill of late afternoon light, so ethereal, filtered through old-growth trees in Wedgwood, a neighborhood of gentle hills and slopes at the edge of strip malls, burger joints, auto dealers, and Rick's topless nightclub in Lake City. But here you never felt you were in a big city—with all those big city problems—because before the Second World War this area used to be an orchard filled with more apple, pear, and plum trees than people, and all that lush plumage absorbed the whoosh of traffic on Lake City Way. Here, traffic moved along at thirty miles per hour. Years ago, it was outside the city limits, and so mailboxes were not attached to our houses but instead were on the street, which had no sidewalks. It's been called a "Prunes and Raisins" neighborhood, but don't ask me why. All I know is that the spirit of place in Wedgwood (this area is named after the English china), where I've lived for half my life, was that of a quiet, hidden oasis within Seattle, inhabited mainly by older, retired people like myself who all owned dogs, and quite a few college professors since it was only two miles from the University of Washington. A wonderful place, if you enjoyed walking. But here and there things had begun to change. Younger people were moving in, and some years ago the police raided a home that someone had turned into a meth lab. Yet and still, such violence in Wedgwood was rare.

So that afternoon, I sat in a lazy Lotus posture under an evergreen tree, the forefingers on each hand tipped against my thumbs, thinking about images from a new poem, "The Ear Is an Organ Made for Love," I'd received via email from my friend Ethelbert Miller, while behind me, floating on an almost hymnal silence, a few soothing notes sounded from the wood chimes hanging from my house, accompanied by bird flutter and the rustle of leaves at about ten decibels. Up above, the light seemed captured in cloud pluffs, which looked luminous, as if they held candles within. Wind soughed in the trees. I began to slowly drift into meditation, hoping today would bring at least a tidbit of spiritual discovery, but no sooner than I'd closed my eyes and felt the outside world fall away, the air was shattered by a hair-raising explosion of music booming from stereo speakers somewhere nearby, like a clap of thunder or a volcano exploding. Now, I love music, especially soft jazz, but only at certain, special hours of the day. This was heavy metal techno—pounding at 120 decibels, alternating with acid rock, and sprinkled with gangster rap that sounded to my ear like rhymed shouting. And it *did* rock—and shock—the neighborhood with a tsunami of inquietude. Its energy was 5 billion times greater than that from the wood chimes. It compressed the air around me and clogged my consciousness. I looked at Nova, and behind his quiet, blackberry eyes he seemed to be thinking, What is *that*, boss?

"Our new neighbors," I said. "We haven't introduced ourselves to them yet, but I guess they're having a party."

You have to understand, I talk to my dog all the time, which is better than talking to myself and being embarrassed if someone caught me doing that, and he never says a word back, which is no doubt one of the reasons why people love dogs.

One or two hours went by, and we listened helplessly as the exhausting, emotionally draining sound yeasted to 130 decibels, moving in concentric spheres from my neighbor's place, covering blocks in every direction like smog or pollution or an oil spill, and just as toxic and rude, as enveloping and inescapable as the Old Testament voice of God when He was having a bad day. And now, suddenly, *I* was having a bad day. This was exactly the opposite of the tranquillity I wanted, but there was no escaping the bass beat that reverberated in my bones, the energy of the shrill profanity and angry lyrics as they assaulted the penetralia of my eardrums, traveling down to the tiny, delicate hairs of the cochlea, and from there to the sensitive sympathetic nervous system that directed the tremors straight into my brain. Unlike an unpleasant vision, from which I could turn away or close my eyes, wave upon wave of oscillations passed right through my hands when I held them against the sides of my head. The music, if I may call it that, was intrusive, infectious, wild, sensual, pagan, orgasmic, jangling, indecent and filled me with foreign emotions not of my own making, completely overwhelming and washing away my thoughts and the silent, inner speech we all experience when our soul talks to itself.

I no longer recognized Wedgwood as my neighborhood. All its virtues—the magnificent views of Lake Washington and the Cascade mountain range, its old-world charm—had vanished, and I felt as if I'd been suddenly teleported to Belltown at eleven o'clock on a Saturday night. I wondered if the Millennial new arrivals to the neighborhood knew how fragile our ears were, and how many scientific studies indicated that noise pollution interfered with learning, lowered math and reading scores, and was responsible for high blood pressure, dry mouth, blindness, muscular contractions, neurosis, heart disease, peptic ulcers, constipation, premature ejaculation, reduced libido, insomnia, congenital birth defects, and even death.

Now darkness had fallen, but still the pulsions continued across the street, surrounding my house like a hand squeezing a wineglass on the verge of shattering. My brain was beginning to feel like one long smear on the inside of my skull. I shook my head at the thought of what a dangerously noisy species we humans are with our clanking, humming, churning machinery and motorcars, our loud music and household appliances with their anapestic beat and fire sirens wailing. Walking into the house, I saw my wife coming down the stairs, wearing her round reading glasses and looking dazed. At sixty-two, she was slightly hard of hearing in one ear, but the stramash had shaken and made her feel exiled from the familiar, too. She started shutting all our windows. But that didn't help. The sound curdled the air inside our house, and her sore ears were burning as bad as mine. From the porch we could see cars lining the street, beer cans thrown into the bushes, and from our neighbor's property there wafted pungent clouds of Purple Haze and Hawaii Skunk marijuana.

"I was reading the Book of Psalms in bed," my wife said, "but I couldn't concentrate with all that noise. What do you think we should do?"

"Call nine-one-one?"

"Oh, no!" she said. Unlike Nova, she *did* talk back to me. "They're just kids. We were kids once, remember?" Then suddenly her lips pouted and she looked hurt. "Why are you shouting at me?"

"Was I shouting?"

"Yes," she said. "You were yelling at me."

I didn't realize how much I'd raised my voice in order to be heard over the mind-blinding music blaring outside—she was, after all, only two feet away from me. Or that the noise, despite all my decades of spiritual practice, could so quickly make me feel spent and flammable and reveal an irascible side of me to my wife neither of us had seen in forty years of marriage. I was no longer myself, though I suspected this was a teachable moment, as politicians say, and there was a lesson to be learned here, but, so help me, I just wasn't getting it. I apologized to my wife. I knew she was right, as usual. We shouldn't call the police. This was a difficult situation that had to be handled with delicacy, but I was confident that I could be as magnanimous and civilized as any post-Enlightenment,

Western man who had control over himself after thirty years of meditation on his mushroom-shaped cushion. But that didn't mean I couldn't try to escape for a while. I decided this was a good time to go shopping. I stepped outside, where the rough, pounding sound almost knocked me to the ground. The traumatizing waves were so thick I felt I was moving through a haze of heat, or underwater. I wondered, Who *are* these rude people? These invaders? I strapped Nova into my Jeep Wrangler, and, with my wife's long list of groceries—milk, canned vegetables, paper towels, a chocolate cake to celebrate the birthday of one of her friends at Mount Zion Baptist Church, and dog treats—in the hip pocket of my jeans, we fled into the night or, more precisely, to the QFC on Thirty-Fifth Avenue.

As the Doppler effect kicked in, as I put half a mile between myself and ground zero, as the pitch declined, I felt less agitated, though there was a slight ringing and seashell sound in my ears, lingering like a low-grade fever. For all the discomfort I was feeling, I also felt something else: namely, how sound and silence, so universal in our lives as to normally be ignored, were profound mysteries I'd never properly understood or respected until now, when the absence of one and the presence of the other were so badly disrupting my life.

Compared to my street, the supermarket, surrounded by eateries and alehouses, was mercifully quiet. I went down the aisles, collecting items we needed, remembering that just one month ago, a QFC employee charged with domestic violence for choking his mother unconscious was killed in this supermarket when he fought the police who came to arrest him. I kept thinking, as I picked items off the shelves, Are those vibes still in this store? (You can probably tell I came of age in the sixties.) I dismissed that thought, and then stood patiently in the checkout line behind five other customers, one being a plump, elderly woman with frosted hair, who, of course, had to pay by writing a check, which seemed to take forever. I swear, I think she was balancing her checking account or calculating her quarterly taxes, there at the front of the line. I could imagine her drinking a hot cup of Ovaltine before going to bed and having ninety-seven cats in her midcentury Wedgwood home. I kept wondering why someone didn't call for another cashier—or even better, two—to handle this line of people backed up into the aisles. Finally, after ten minutes it was my turn. The cashier was a genial young man whose eyes behind his wire-framed glasses looked glazed from ringing up so many customers, but he was trying to be cheerful. He took my QFC Advantage card and said, "So how is *your* day going?"

Usually, I enjoy chatting with people behind the cash register, finding out a little about their lives, letting them know they're people in my community I care about and not just faceless objects to me. I try to be patient, reciting my mantra if I have a long wait in a public place. But right then I said, in spite of myself, "What the hell do you care?"

That reply shocked him as much as it did me. I tried to recover. I said, "Sorry! I didn't *mean* that. I think I'm vibrating too fast."

He cut his eyes my way. "Excuse me?"

"Long story . . . Never mind."

"You want paper or plastic?"

My voice wobbled. "Paper . . . please."

That would prove to be a mistake.

Then I hurried out of QFC, pushing my little gray cart with four bags of groceries as quickly as I could, and stopped at Rite Aid across the street to buy earplugs for my wife and myself. It was now nine-thirty P.M. Driving home, I was praying the neighbor's party was over, but to my surprise, yet somehow not to my surprise, I felt the density in the schizy air before I heard the humping arcs still flooding the neighborhood like a broken water main. Even worse, when I downshifted into my driveway, I had to hit the brakes because another car was parked in *my* space. My neighbor's guests had filled the street with their vehicles. The one in my driveway, a Chevrolet Blazer, had a skull-and-bones decal in the back window, and under that a bumper sticker that said YOU CAN KISS THE CRACK BELOW MY BACK. My first impulse was to let the air out of its tires, but then I realized that would only keep it in my driveway even longer.

So I parked two blocks away. I looped Nova's nylon lease around my left wrist, loaded up my arms as high as my chin with four heavy bags of food, and started tramping slowly uphill to my house. That's when fat raindrops began to fall. By the time I was thirty feet from my front door, the paper bags were soaking wet and falling apart. Ten feet from the front door, Nova realized we were almost home. He sprang forward for the steps—Westies hate to get wet—and that snapped my left arm straight out, which sent cans of sliced pineapples, soup, and tomatoes, bottles of maple syrup and milk, and bags of raisins, potatoes, and rice cascading back down the declivity, littering the street like confetti or a landfill. For the longest time, I stood there, head tipped and sopping wet, watching my neighbor's guests flee inside to escape the rain, lost in the whorl of violent, invisible vibrations, and I was disabused forever of the vanity that three decades of practicing meditation had made me too civilized, too cultivated, too mellow to be vulnerable to or victimized by fugitive thoughts—anger, desire, self-pity, pettiness—triggered in me from things outside. These would always arise, I saw, even without noise pollution.

Then, all at once, the loud music stopped.

Dragging my dog behind me, I slogged across the street, so tired I couldn't see straight. I climbed my new neighbor's stairs, and banged my fist on the front door. After a moment it opened, and standing there with a can of Budweiser in his right hand was possibly the most physically fit young man I'd ever seen. I placed his age at thirty. Maybe thirty-five. His short hair was a military buzz cut, his T-shirt olive-colored, his ears large enough for him to wiggle if he wanted to, like President Obama's, and on his arm I saw a tattoo for the Fourth Brigade of the Second Infantry Division he'd served with at Joint Base Lewis-McChord. He looked me up and down as I stood dripping on his doorstep, and politely said:

"Yes, sir? Can I help you?"

"We need to talk," I said.

He squinted his eyes as if trying to read my lips. Then he put one hand behind his ear like an old, old man who'd lost his hearing aid, or someone who'd been a blacksmith all his life. "What did you say, sir?"

I was less than a foot away from him. I felt like I was awakening from a dream. A profound sadness swept over me, dousing my anger, for I understood the unnecessary tragedy of tinnitus in someone so young. His was maybe the result of a recent tour in Iraq or Afghanistan, perhaps from an IED. I felt humbled. I did not judge him or myself now, because he had taught me how to listen better. I gestured with one finger held up for him to wait a moment, and went back out into the downpour. On the street, I found one of the items, protected by a plastic lid. I climbed the steps again.

"Thank you," I said, giving him the chocolate cake. "And welcome to Wedgwood."

Guinea Pig

I was a student at the University of Washington in Seattle, with a double major in philosophy and English, those two broken and declining (if not already dead) fields in higher education, and by the end of my third year I was going broke and couldn't afford both tuition and food, but because I was physically healthy (mentally is a different matter), I started selling my vital fluids to the blood bank, and volunteering for every science experiment conducted on campus, and even off campus, by aspiring inventors, provided they paid the participants.

So instead of preparing for my classes this fall, I'm sitting in a chair amiddlemost a laboratory longer than it is wide, lit overhead by soft fluorescent bulbs beneath the ceiling of one of the science buildings funded by the Bill & Melinda Gates Foundation. Their largesse is visible everywhere on campus, but especially here in the high-tech labs and über state-of-the-art scientific equipment. Miles of cables like a nest of boa constrictors are hidden away behind the walls, ceiling, and floor. Flasks and burners in the lab are interspersed with a warren of monitors, scanners that in seconds can read every chemical beneath the casement of your skin, then spit forth a fire hose of data into devices that compute a thousand times faster than human thought. Two technicians of twenty-five and thirty, very polite, are making last-minute adjustments. I've been calling them Alphonse and Gaston because one is tall with a stiff, sliding way of walking, while the other is bald, has a belly that bubbles over his belt, and keeps a goofy little grin plastered on his face.

In the middle of this elaborate machine, this triumph of the Enlightenment, on a rainy evening in October, we're waiting for Dr. Samantha Conner to signal the start of her experiment, and on the brink of being ambushed by X-rated revelations no stuffy philosophy seminar can provide. I'm guessing she is thirty-five, a workaholic, single, the sort of brainy woman who won prize after prize at science fairs in middle school, a child prodigy who skipped high school, started at MIT when she was thirteen, earned a MacArthur Fellowship before she was old enough for a driver's license, and had no time for something as frivolous as boys or dating because she still had to prove herself over and over in the higher echelons of the rigorous hard sciences, where members of her gender are too few and far between. For me, a lowly, financially ludicrous philosophy geek in the unscientific, subjective world of literary studies, Dr. Conner, as she studies some head-breaking equation on her clipboard, is so heartbreakingly beautiful she makes my eyes blur, like maybe I'm looking at Gwyneth Paltrow in a white lab coat, gold-framed glasses over leaf-green eyes, with fawn-like ears, a nose turned up at the tip, and hair pinned behind her neck by a wooden comb. I guess I've always had a serious case of slide-rule envy. Cerebral women with IQs over 170 have always been catnip for me, the way mountain climbers are drawn to the Matterhorn. I just fall apart in their presence. And I knew my desire for her was not just painful but also impossible. By the way the world reckoned things, I was a loser headed for the night shift at McDonald's. ("Would you like fries with that and a definition of *agape*?") Microsoft didn't need a resident metaphysician. And a bachelor's degree in English was about as good as one in basket weaving. Nevertheless, I had a theory that all those messy, bottled-up feelings and the wild, sensual joy celebrated in the sloppy humanities but repressed in the sciences by quantification and reducing everything to the crystalline clarity of numbers just might under the right conditions explode like a truckload of Chinese fireworks.

During my interview, my heart did get ahead of me. I asked Dr. Conner if she'd have dinner with me at Faire Gallery Café on Capitol Hill, despite the differences in our ages, bank accounts, and academic rank. The blistering stare she gave me, peering over the rim of her spectacles, was paralyzing, like maybe I was something toxic she was looking at in a petri dish—English and philosophy majors get this kind of Godzilla-eyeball all the time.

I told her, "I'm a lot smarter than you think."

"You'd have to be," she said, spanking me for taking such liberties above my station.

Cold and efficient, she avoided my romantic overture. But I could sense how important this new study would be for her career. She said it was based on work conducted in 2008 at the Karolinska Institute in Stockholm by Valeria Petkova and her colleague Henrik Ehrsson. These two called it the "body-swap illusion." Their test subjects wore a shiny black helmet that favored ones used in football minus the face guard, and sat across from other people or mannequins like the crash dummies used to test air bags in cars, and after just a few moments of being rigged up like that, they shook hands and experienced the mind-warping sensation that they had suddenly switched bodies with those others. In a word, the illusion was that they were lifted out of themselves, however briefly, freed from the tight Cartesian cage that always held the self cloistered, locked in solitary confinement as a lonely monad forever separate from other unreachable monads—as I was from Samantha Conner—ontologically isolated, solipsistic, drifting through life with the rest of the world, its objects and others, always "over there." Their work promised to be a new tool for exploring that greatest of all mysteries, self-identity; for breaking down the epistemological apartheid of mind-body dualism; and for enhancing virtual reality experiences.

But here's the trick:

Dr. Conner and her technicians won't use a lifeless mannequin. Or even another person. No, she dismissed that as being too easy. Too tame. She told me she had always been a nonconformist, an explorer in pursuit of the extraordinary, a person who questioned authority, and rejected any rules that held women back in a patriarchal society. Since childhood, Samantha had always looked at familiar things as if they were strange, and strange things as if they were familiar. She was congenitally disposed to always challenge conventions, the pedestrian, the predictable, the mundane, and go where others feared to go. I swear, her spirit of adventure and imagination stirred me up like music. Because she tilted toward innovation and breaking taboos (and also because, to my knowledge, she hadn't published a scientific paper in five years), she said my companion in her raising the stakes on Petkova's study would not even be human.

He's sitting right in front of me now, a 130-pound Rottweiler named Casey, her dog: lazily licking his paws, and wearing a black helmet just like the one I'm holding in my hands. It covers his eyes and pointed ears, and displays a 3-D version of what the other participant sees. In other words, what *I* see. I wasn't surprised that she was uncommonly fond of her dog, and selected him to be my partner. People in Seattle are so in love with this species they probably spell its name, dog, backwards, and why not? Canines and humans have a 75 percent overlap between their genetic codes. From one of my seminars on Plato's *Republic*, I remembered that in Book Two, Socrates praised dogs for being high-spirited lovers of wisdom. So, yeah, I was okay with dogs, those symbols of fidelity. But I'm wondering, you know, how all this is going to turn out, if maybe I should have told her about some of the other, bizarre experiments for which I'd been a human guinea pig, if maybe all *that* might somehow prove to be an X factor neither she nor I had figured on. Maybe when I signed the consent form, which elaborated on the possible side effects of this experiment, but also pointed out that some consequences were unpredictable and might cause death, maybe I should have told her then in that tiny office of hers, with a wall of awards, the sawdust smell of new books, and a view of Lake Washington, that some of those government-funded studies I survived won or were finalists for the Ig Nobel Prizes, handed out for the most ridiculous scientific research conducted every year.*

Over a period of two years, I participated in experiments that measured people's brainwave patterns while they chewed different colored M&M's. In another experiment I was tested to determine if University of Washington males were more sexually attracted to UW females than to tennis balls—we were, according to the findings, but only marginally. I was the test subject for a musical condom that contained a microchip like the ones in musical greeting cards—when used, it played the 1812 Overture and Handel's *Messiah*. And I will never forget

---

* Examples of Ig Nobel Prize winners are taken from *The Ig Nobel Prizes: The Annals of Improbable Research* by Marc Abrahams (Dutton, 2002). Dog facts are from Stephen Budiansky's *The Truth About Dogs* (Penguin, 2000) and Stanley Coren's *How Dogs Think* (Free Press, 2004).

the bumps I got on my head from a study called "Injuries Due to Falling Coconuts"; or the survey I was in about human belly button lint—who gets it, when, what color, and how much.

"Jeremy," said Dr. Conner, tapping the end of her nose with a pencil. "Are you ready?"

"Yes, ma'am." I sat up straight in my chair. "I think so."

The shiny plastic helmet was as light as Styrofoam in my hands. It would cover everything except my mouth. Slowly, I slid it over my head, plunging the room into darkness as black as onyx. I could faintly hear voices around me, Dr. Conner and her two technicians, but the world was void, without form or light for the longest time, as it must have been in the nanoseconds before the Big Bang. So far all right. I felt Alphonse throw a switch on the side of my helmet. It began to hum. But then, unbeknownst to the others, some kind of circuit went haywire. Inside the helmet my nostrils caught a whiff of smoke, then pain like a burning wire stabbed through my temples. I winced, and held my breath, but I didn't let on that anything might be wrong because I wanted full payment for my participation in this so I didn't want them to terminate it prematurely.

Gradually and by degrees, the pain subsided. On the screen inside my helmet I began to see spicules of light, but I was color-blind. I could only see things sharply if they were about a foot away. The character of the lab had changed into a soft-focus watercolor of washed-out blues and pale yellows, as if everything was covered by a diaphanous piece of cellophane smeared with Vaseline. But what I was suddenly lacking in depth of field was more than compensated for by the tone-color of all that I could smell angling across the air—Gaston, I realized, had a few recreational drugs and a dime bag of cannabis in his lab coat (the excellent herb called Hawaii Maui Wowie), which I guess explained why he was always grinning; and Alphonse, whether he knew it or not, was carrying in his wallet fives, tens, and twenties scented with just a trace of cocaine, which can be found on nine out of ten bills in the United States. Then, as I turned my head, I saw a hazy, helmeted shape, larger than myself, hairless (which struck me as very odd), and wearing a white T-shirt emblazoned with the slogan CONSCIOUSNESS: THAT ANNOYING TIME BETWEEN NAPS. It was a totally ridiculous-looking, two-legged creature without a tail, chicken-necked, with thin, unmuscled arms, not good for anything, as far as I could see, except maybe rubbing your tummy or opening doors so you could go outside. Only at that instant did I realize it was me seen from Casey's side of the room. Not just through the camera in his helmet, but through the exotic difference of his mind as he experienced the roomscape as an explosion of odors sweet and pungent, subtle and gross, moist and dry, everything elemental, not lensed through language, not weakened by a web of words, not muddled by culture or cultivation. I heard a collage of sounds I could pinpoint the location for in one eighteen-thousandth of a second, sounds four octaves higher than humans can perceive: the world as it might be known to an extraterrestrial from the Zeta Reticuli star system. Then Dr. Conner said, *Go ahead, you two, Jeremy, Casey, shake hands.*

When I lifted, then planted what felt like my black-padded paw in the palm of whoever that pathetically deaf, nose-dead creature was over there, when I touched myself touching, I was completely in Casey's body, he in mine: two entangled electrons. All at once, the world became new, a place of mystery and the uncanny, the way a two-year-old sees it, and strangest of all was my knowing there had to *already* be a bit of the canine in me, and the *Homo sapiens* in Casey, for the experiment to work in the first place. The doctor was more successful than she knew. For just this moment, not only did it feel like we'd switched bodies, but our minds had commingled, too.

And then, as abruptly as it began, the experiment was over.

I felt Gaston lifting off my helmet. For an instant the light in the lab blinded me. I kept blinking and saw through fluttering eyelids Dr. Conner leaning toward me, using one finger to push her glasses higher on her nose toward her glabella.

"How do you feel?" she said. "Describe what happened."

I wasn't sure I could. Yes, the body-swap illusion was over. But having been freed from my skin, after stepping outside a fixed idea of myself, I couldn't exactly find my way back in, as if inside and outside, here and there, had always been the real illusion and I just never noticed it before now. Thanks to Dr. Conner's experiment, I could no longer tell, in terms of the big picture, where I ended and others began.

Can you?

Yet, she and the technicians still *did* look faintly like a different species to me, as strange as snakes or snails. Involuntarily, I started scratching myself. And for some reason I felt more cagey, manipulative, and as playful as a puppy.

"It worked just like you said it would," I told her. "Just like it did at the Karolinska Institute. You know, I think you're going to get a Nobel Prize."

"Really? You do?" Her eyes crinkled at the thought, and that wrinkled her nose. "Why?"

"Well, there was some kind of short in the helmet's circuitry, and—and even before we shook hands, the switch happened, I mean it *really* happened, not with our bodies, but our thoughts."

"Thoughts? That's not possible," she said. "Can you prove that?"

"Okay." I drew a deep breath. "Just before you turned things off, I got an image from Casey, evanescent but a clear picture in my mind . . ."

"Of what?"

"Does your bedroom have a print of Picasso's *Three Musicians* on the wall, over the bed?"

"Yes."

"And a blue, corduroy bedspread?"

Her eyebrows rose. "Yes, I bought that last year."

"And you listen to George Clinton music on your iPod?"

"Yes—yes, I do." She cut her eyes at me. "Jeremy, where is this going?"

"Well, I saw you on that bed. George Clinton's 'Atomic Dog' was playing. Some nights you let Casey sleep close by in the corner. And you always sleep in the buff. You've got the cutest mole on your abdomen, and this really great honeypot tattoo on the upper, inner part of your left thigh . . ."

Dr. Conner cupped her right hand over my mouth. I'd never seen anyone move so quickly. Alphonse and Gaston looked round at her in wonder. The doctor's cheeks flushed cherry pink.

"That's just a carryover from college and too many margaritas one night." She laughed, her voice quivering. "I think Jeremy may need to rest awhile. Why don't you two take a coffee break."

I pulled her hand down and said, "No, I'm fine. I like to sleep in the buff too. And then there's that *other* tattoo on . . ."

Samantha's clipboard fell clattering to the floor, and she hissed at Alphonse and Gaston, "Leave. *Now!*"

They hurried out of the room, and when she swung her head back toward me, I was so mesmerized by the beauty of the golden highlights in her hair that, in spite of myself, a new impulse took hold of me.

I licked her face.

That sent her backpedaling about five feet, holding the wet spot as if she'd been stung. And now she had a spot of lipstick on her front tooth. After a moment, Samantha composed herself. She smoothed down her black skirt, picked up her clipboard, found her pencil, and was again the portrait of professionalism, taking notes in her obsessively neat and idiosyncratic script, her *T*s like the Space Needle, her *M*s like an outline of the Cascades.

"Is there anything *else,* Jeremy?" Her eyes were evasive. "These perceptual and behavioral transformations are, um, unprecedented. I want to know everything."

Actually, she did not want to know *every*thing, so I thought it best not to tell her that, like Casey, I had an overwhelming urge to sniff her butt, something with which she would not approve, of course, but in his case and mine it was just in the disinterested pursuit of gathering information, you understand.

"Oh, there's a lot more," I said. "You're going to have enough new research for publications to last a lifetime. Naturally, I'm at your service for any further experiments, conferences, or lectures you'll be called upon to do. You know, as living proof of your success with interspecies communications. I can also help you translate technical jargon into proper English, which will make your research reader-friendly for a larger, public audience, especially with dog lovers. That means more popularity for you and easier fund-raising. You might even need to start an institute. But sorting all this out will take a while. I'd say days. Even weeks or years. Maybe we can start by you letting me take you to dinner." I was still trying to bridge the gap between the arts and sciences.

I saw her shoulders relax. She lowered her clipboard to her side, and experimented with a smile. Just as I was seeing things anew, I could tell by the tilt of her head that she was perhaps seeing Jeremy Tucker, English and philosophy major, for the first time.

"So much about you *is* different now," she said. "You seem much more useful and . . . *feral*. Yes, I think perhaps we can do dinner. I'll bring a tape recorder."

I figured we had enough to discuss for a lifetime, and who knows where things might go from there? But this is where my fabliau (I believe that's the right form, I aced a class on the genre) ends, one I hope caused no offense, but if it did, try to keep in mind that sometimes every able-bodied American male enjoys being a dog.

4189

CHARLES JOHNSON AND STEVEN BARNES

Anticipation [of death] reveals to [the I-self] its lostness in the they-self, and brings it face to face with the possibility of being itself, primarily unsupported by concernful solicitude, but of being itself, rather, in an impassioned ***freedom towards death***—a freedom which has been released from the Illusions of the "they," and which is factical, certain of itself, and anxious.

—Martin Heidegger, *Being and Time*

We shed the bulky, vanilla-colored coveralls worn on the Möbius line. Ferris bids the kiva surround us with breathtaking Northwest forest, green petals, and needles gleaming with dew. They shiver when caressed by the wind, as Ferris does when the tip of my tongue traces circles around her pebble-like nipples. Just visible in the distance, she has called forth an abandoned wooden Soto Zen temple, the kind once seen everywhere in Japan. When there still *was* a Japan.

Age, even decay, has made it strangely beautiful and somehow precious in its impermanence.

Ferris enjoys coupling in settings such as this, where spirit commingles with flesh, echoes of a time when life died from the day it was born.

We drop naked onto layers of leaves covering the forest floor. I open the thumb-size vial of Thanadose. A month's salary moving between chits to barter to black market through cutouts and burned bridges. Illegal as self-murder, and worth every erg.

Ferris tilts her head back, sipping from the vial. I follow her lead. Then, as the serum takes effect, we kiss hungrily, salty-mint syrup coating our tongues. For a time the microsynthes crawling through our veins stop whispering *eternity* and we can glimpse an ending, as did our ancestors. Back before we knew we were male or female, knew only that sexual sweetness banished, however briefly, fear of the eternal night.

Sweetness, in the shadow of the worm.

After a year of trysts, we know each other's heats and tastes and textures. I can play her exactly as she wishes to be played.

She is drop-dead beautiful, as perfect as a pleasure doll. Could have an Upper if she wished. A mere fluke of genetics that she was born Lower. A fluke of luck that she wants me.

First, I push back her nut-brown, shoulder-length hair. I slowly trace my tongue along her neck, beneath her small delicate ears, where a vein dances with life. She closes her eyes and sighs, as if drifting into sleep, but it is actually shameless surrender, luxuriating in every elemental, spasm-inducing sensation I stroke up through the envelope of her skin. She trusts me completely. We keep touching until touching becomes inebriation and our eyes begin to blur. Then my left hand parts her legs. Ferris lifts her knees, and I bury my face where her vulva and labia are moist and lathered, layered like the inside of a flower. She trembles until she is carried away, far away, returning to me with her fingers tangled gratefully in my hair, her eyes bright as stars.

At last, I slide into the warmth and wetness of her. She grips at me with her inner muscles, locking so tightly I can barely move. Then releasing so that we churn, melting into one another, and finally lie in each other's arms, sipping one another's breath.

It is all there is, but as the Thanadose fades, the sweetness recedes. I try to hold the illusion: *I will die. Everything ends. This moment is all we have . . .*

But no, it is a lie. We are untouched by time. We will have tomorrow, and tomorrow, and every tomorrow thereafter. No one knows how long those who remain on planet Earth will live. Perhaps forever. That would horrify me. If I felt horror.

But I do not. Or, as Thanadose fades, love. Only the body and its microsynthes, whirring on, eternal.

We are left with after-quakes. We are told that that is enough. That this is all there is.

I don't believe that anymore. And that is a sin.

* * *

Sweat cools.

"La petite mort," she whispered.

"What?"

"The small death." Her finger traced a figure eight on my chest.

"Some kind of Upper talk?" Beautiful as she is, I'd not be surprised if she had a lover across the divide. Perhaps she'd been a courtesan, demoted to the Möbius line for reasons I might never know. You could see it in the little things that betrayed her breeding, like the way she walked and talked and smiled, feminine in every fiber and almost too perfect to believe. Her elegant gestures, her perfectly pronounced speech, and elite Upper education, none of which she could hide. All that would explain some of the things she said, but not whatever it was she saw in me.

"Hundreds of years ago, the French referred to an orgasm as the 'little death.'" She pressed herself closer to me, somehow a greater intimacy than that which had gone before.

"The French?" I said.

"That was when there was a France." She shrugged, then kissed my shoulder.

I gave a headshake, yes. Now, of course, there is no France, or England or Germany. Or much of anything else outside our domed polises, each sustaining 10 million perfectly regulated lives, the city-state that is mother and father to us all. We could thank the Food Wars for that, and leveling the planet's population to 100 million. And these days only "little" deaths seem to exist at all. I'd never thought about things like that before Ferris.

She was supposed to have been relief. Just physical release from the monotony of working the line.

She had opened my eyes.

Not like the other women I'd had over the last . . . I don't know how long. At least a hundred and sixty years. We are discouraged from thinking about years and serial relationships long past and replaceable. Days, minutes, yes. And we're encouraged not to forget the communal wisdom of the polis, *I am because we are*. No single person is special or unique. Except . . .

Ferris *is* special to me, I think. I want her forever and that is forbidden.

I have lost count of my years, or sex partners. I could place them all on a chorus line that would stretch a quarter mile, their faces blurring together. But Ferris is more. She is the lover who might save me from myself. For her I take risks. The Thanadose she brings to us could cost me status on the line. I could be demoted. It has taken me ten years to work my way up to assessment, off the assembly queue, repairing whatever is sent us.

But . . . if I lose something, it is worth it. She is worth it.

I can't exactly say she loves me. Or that I love her. "Love" died during the Wars, like so many things. But this—whatever it is—is all we have, and more than I expected. It may be as much as the Uppers have, and that thought makes me smile.

*　　*　　*

We parted with a promise, but not a kiss. She retired to her sleep kiva, and I to mine. A sleeping place, living place, eating place. There are public eateries, parks, museums. They belong to all. We have all we need.

I enjoy cooking. After tubing home in our domed anthill, I spent some ergs and had fresh chicken waiting on the conveyor. Spent the evening experimenting with tastes and textures, and consumed my dinner alone, facing the framed picture of Ferris on my wall. She does not know I have it.

Perhaps I would invite Ferris to my home. It would be a big step. Perhaps one day we would ask for a contract, for a year or a decade. Whatever I could get.

I dreamed of her.

It is not love. But it is what I have.

*　　*　　*

Dreams are carefully monitored and directed, lyrical, speaking of life and hope. No nightmares (Ferris told me of those), no chasings or fallings. No flying, either.

I make a promise to tube out to the Pacific, where the transparent dome (so like photos I've seen of terrariums) that separates us from the toxic air outside ends. I would take a room, just sit by a window and watch the roll of pewter-gray waves beneath a blue and bottomless sky. That would be good. Nothing out there lives in the hazy atmosphere, but watching the roily, ever-changing water would bring a bit of tranquillity to my brooding, as I sometimes do, on the waxing and waning of world civilizations.

Morning comes.

Tubing in to work is pleasant, rolling through the parks. There are many, and they are all beautiful. I see the night shift playing and strolling. Some play with pets. Once upon a time I saw pictures of children playing in the park. I actually saw a child once, a tangled-haired little girl. Why her Caregiver took her outside the children's sector is beyond me. I wonder if having children would be more . . . satisfying . . . than pets. I would never know such luxury. Or know anyone who had.

Children grow, and change, in a world where change has been banished to the shadows. So they are elsewhere. Where, I don't know. I know I was a child once, but remember little of that time save playing with my crèchemates. I remember liking chocolate ice cream. I cannot stand it now.

Somewhere out there, the Uppers live. I've only heard rumors about them, strange, contradictory stories. Some say their lives are decadent and devoted to unnatural pleasures, others claim they are old-fashioned, cultivated, with close-knit families, no making love before marriage with anything other than sex dolls, and even going twice a day to temples to worship a god whose name is too holy for them to utter, and whose image, if drawn or otherwise depicted, is an offense punishable by memory wipe. On some days, when the sky is very clear, I can see their towers. Kilometers high, beautiful as death.

That is wrong. Death is not beautiful. Life is beautiful. I have heard that since always. I should go to the psyops and ask for a correction.

*　　*　　*

Work is as it always is. A machine I had not seen before came down the line. When I researched its fixing, I found that it was like a type of marine chronometer seen now only in the antique military craft sometimes used in Upper games of war, where people pretend to die. I pulled it from the line, and spent half the day exploring, and renewing the thing. Robots could do any of what I did, and maybe even better, but except for household bots, machines doing the supposedly ennobling work of men and women were abolished long ago. When the chronometer pulsed to life again, I put it back on the line, where it mysteriously went on to whatever destination it would ultimately have, off the line. Where did it go? One doesn't ask about what goes on before or after the station where one stands every day.

At dinner, I saw Ferris. She sat alone in the dining room, which was lined with cooking stations, and the endless buffet. Food is wonderful. I love it.

I sat with her, and she acknowledged me with a nod. She seemed withdrawn, staring at a tendriled flaw in her wineglass, an indentation shaped like a starburst. I asked her if she would see me tonight, and she shook her head.

"Why?"

"I want more"—her voice quivered—"we were so close. So close."

"Yes." I nodded, knowing what she meant, how we carried eternity within ourselves like an ache or soreness in our muscles. "We were."

"It was like stepping right to the edge of a cliff"—her eyes slipped out of focus as she thought about it—"looking down and feeling the ground beckoning me to step out into space, into bliss, then we backed away at the last moment . . ."

I just stared at her, afraid to speak.

"Shane, don't run away from what I'm saying. Don't look away when I'm talking to you! We *have* to do this." Her gaze snapped back, locking into mine, refusing to let go. Her voice was barely above a whisper. "We have to die. Together."

*   *   *

Hours later, back in my sleep kiva, I could still feel the thrill that flooded through me when Ferris had the courage to give voice to thoughts still unformed in my own mind. I lacked the courage to formulate them fully, let alone put them into words. *We had to die.* It was as simple as that. Together, at the height of our lovemaking and passion, we would taste extinction and real eternity.

Death. Forbidden fruit. The one tree we were warned not to touch.

I let the idea unwind, wondering what it would be like to nibble at this. I stepped into the spotless kitchen, where every stain and odor, sweet or offensive, was obliterated by roaming microsynthe colonies. From the cutlery cabinet, I withdrew the biggest, sharpest blade I could find. I paused for a moment. All my life I'd been what others wanted me to be. I'd bent or broken little rules here and there, sure. Everyone did that. It was expected. But I'd never toyed with anything taboo. Not until now. Trembling, taking a deep breath, and with just a single stroke, I cleanly sliced open my left wrist right to the bone. Blood . . . It should have geysered from the ugly gash I opened. But the microsynthes work with abominable speed. As if in a dream, I stared at my wrist as they worked, repairing me, removing even the individuating scar that would have distinguished me from everyone else in the polis. Suddenly, I felt a scream spasm up through my throat. I could have cut off my entire hand, but I would have just been printed another, identical one from my genome file.

I wanted—needed—to bleed. To feel that *some*thing changes. And matters. To wake up from this nightmare of forever.

We must die. I knew that then. But in order to do that we had to find the Death Dealers.

*   *   *

I spent the next day denying that the conversation had ever taken place, but it lingered like a low-grade fever. How could I believe it? Suspended between hope and horror, I went to the line, and worked. I didn't see Ferris at lunch, and then I saw her and she wouldn't talk to me. I knew her reason. Disgust with my own cowardice overwhelmed me. I wrote her a note, and tucked it under one of the flanges of a drum of combined African and Korean design, destined for Ferris's line.

"I will try," it said.

Heard nothing back from her, and slept that night alone, and lonely. Awakened in the middle of the night, and sent a message to the single-use drop Billy had given me twenty years ago.

She was in the cafeteria the next day, her hair gathered up in a coil, but seemed tetchy and again would not speak to me. Her eyes bled need and want.

The next day I merely rambled through the motions, feeling emotionally murky, when a repair job came in, the one I had been waiting for. Tied with a red ribbon. It felt as if a weight had been lifted from my chest, and in the cafeteria I managed to get her to take my hand, and passed her a note: *"Tonight."*

She came to my table, eyes brimming with gratitude.

"My brother says he can help us," I said.

Playfully, she raised an eyebrow and pouted her lips. "Is that a pie crust promise?"

"Huh?"

"Easy to make and easy to break." Ferris winked at me. "*Thank* you. I knew you wouldn't let me down." Then she did something she had never done before: she leaned over, held my head in both hands, and kissed me. A few of the others looked over, curious. Public displays of physical affection were rare.

"It's going to be so good," she whispered. She was glowing. Her cheeks. Lips. Totally turned on. She took me by the hand to a comfort room, peeled my clothes off, and welded her body to mine.

She was like a furnace, insatiable. It had never been like that before. And would never be again.

*   *   *

How do you dress for death? What do you leave for others to find?

An autopod took me to a side street where Ferris waited at the entrance to a tattoo parlor. Streetlamps penciled a latticework of patterns on the moving sidewalk in front of her. Behind her, animated tats of constellations and extinct animals blossomed on the skin of living models in the windows: a gam of whales spewed columns of water skyward, a brace of eagles spread their wings, elephants thundered. Dead now, like death itself.

The pod's doors sighed open. Once she was inside, the windows blacked out.

"The pod?" she asked.

"Off the grid," I said. "Cost a lot of ergs, but can't be traced."

That seemed to reassure her. Closing her eyes, she leaned into me, her head of flush, nut-brown hair on my shoulder. "It won't matter after tonight."

"No," I said. "It won't."

In silence, then. The pod glided on as Ferris dozed. I'd told her little about my crèchemate Billy, how we'd been raised together, but walked different paths. He was sly, crafty. He'd spent time as a cop, a psych tech, a street maintenance guy. Now . . . well, I didn't know how he made money, and I'm not sure I'd want to. But from time to time we still exchanged favors. Now, he was going to grant me one final request.

Finally, after what seemed like hours, we came to a busy rialto close to a different zone. A kind of tenderloin market-place abutting the upper-class zone. Judging by sound and sensation we descended into a tunnel. Long narrow drive. Then we stopped. The interior lights came on. The doors opened. Ferris and I climbed out. The autopod moved away in the direction it had come, plunging us into woolly cave-like darkness. Ferris held my hand tightly, her palms slick with moisture.

As our eyes gradually adjusted to this chamber, I realized we'd been deposited in a death brothel. Until now, I'd only heard about places like these, a hair-raising edge zone, liminal, where Uppers and Lowers shed their assigned status and met secretly for every sort of illegal sex. Faintly, as shapes came into focus in a common space that connected to a warren of private rooms, I saw death and twisted Venusian embraces commingled in exhibitionistic ecstasy. Instantly, I felt ill. Naked men wanting to be watched were grinding against women painted to resemble corpses. Others sat in shadowed cubbyholes twitching and jerking and erect, neural helmets playing end-of-life brain waves. Women coupled with aged surrogates and grunting beasts. Men gripped and thrust into things that looked as if they were barely . . . barely . . .

My god, my eyes had to have been lying. The tiny bodies and disproportionate heads, the mewling screams . . . they *had* to have been clones, or dolls, or . . .

My brain felt on the edge of shutdown, refusing to process what I was seeing. The scent of sex mingled with the stench of decomposition. The room rushed at me, then receded. I felt dizzy, and came within a hash mark of fainting, but Ferris was so stimulated she could hardly stand. Even in this sexual abattoir, her musk was a tangible thing. Off to our left, I saw a door. Before it stood a husky, hairy-necked, masked man, ponderous and pale as a ghost. He wore cutaway pants, exposing chalky flesh. Hermaphrodite, with a hard distended belly like a sack of marbles. Not far from him, a drooling woman crawled along the floor, eyes ripped from her face. Empty sockets swarmed with microsynthes, already knitting new orbs.

"I saw it," she moaned. "Can't *you* see it?"

Suddenly and without a sound, Billy materialized at my side.

"Shane," he said.

"Billy." I took a breath and with two fingers wiped sweat off my forehead. "You startled me."

He looked much like me. Dark knotted hair, dusky copper skin. Eternally at his physical peak. Squint lines around bright eyes that had seen too much, for too long. Pimp, go-between, facilitator. My crèche brother.

"You always were jumpy, Shane. More nervous than anyone else in our litter. Never figured I'd see you in a place like this." His brown, heavy-lidded eyes, which deceptively always made him seem sleepy when he was, in fact, alert to everything going on, swung toward Ferris, as if he was appraising a nice veal chop on his kiva's conveyor. "She the one?"

"She's the one," I said.

His lips twisted up in a smile. "You always had luck with good-lookin' ladies, brother. Sometimes I hated you for that." I hadn't seen Billy in thirty years, but our childhood bond was strong enough for me to read his expression, despite his carefully guarded emotions. In childhood, Billy had always covered my back when anyone tried to mess with me or when I looked like I was about to do something stupid. Like maybe now.

"Can't talk you out of this?"

"Uh-uh."

"Okay, it's your funeral."

When I looked confused by that, Ferris gently applied pressure to my hand and said, "Back when people died, their friends and family would get together with their dead bodies, all cleaned up, and say nice things about them."

As always, I took Ferris at her word, and turned back to Billy.

"All my possessions and kiva go into a trust." I handed him a plastic card. "This is the code. If I . . . when I die, you get everything. It's not much, but I owe you."

"You *do*." He blinked, greed overriding brotherly love. "Miss you, my friend."

I tried to smile, and couldn't quite manage.

Billy gave Ferris a slow look sideways, his face suddenly suspicious. "You an Upper? Don't lie. I can hear it in your voice."

"No. But . . . I spent time there in childhood."

He gazed into her eyes. I had seen the horrors of the outer room, and knew that to be nothing compared to what Billy had to know. He could imagine things beyond my mind. But even with so much history behind him, he had a lot of heart. Sympathy softened suspicion. "And . . . this is what you want, sister? You go into this, you don't come out, ever."

"I want it." She nodded. "With all my heart."

"In that case . . . then, here it is." He extended a closed fist and opened it. There were two pills in his palm, one blue, one pink.

"What is this?" I asked.

"One for each of you. She takes the pink pill, naturally. You take the blue. Or . . . you would, if I were to give you these. But that would be against the law, wouldn't it?"

I stared at them, there in the hollow of his hand. "If I did . . . if we did take these, what would happen?"

"Well, they are binary neurotoxins coupled with micro-synthe antagonists."

"And . . . we'll die?"

"If you make love, yes. The microsynthes are triggered by sexual brain-wave patterns." He managed a crooked smile and chuckled. "Literally, you'd *come* and *go* at the same time—get it?—but only with each other."

"Why?" Ferris asked.

He shrugged. "More romantic that way, I guess. Don't ask me. I don't make this shit. I just sell it." Billy dropped both pills in front of us.

I picked up mine, looked at it. The echoes of sex, pain, and simulated death filled my ears. Moans. Cries. As if even more unspeakable things were happening just outside of my sight.

Terrible.

Ferris rolled her pill around in her hand. "We take these home?"

Billy shook his head. "If I knew what you were talking about, which I don't, I'd say no. They don't leave here. Take them here, or not at all."

I was shaking, trembling all over. "What happens to . . ."

"Your bodies?" A ghost of a terrible smile. "We waste nothing."

Thoughts formed, crashed against each other, dissolved. There were no more decisions to make. "Good-bye, Billy. Thank you."

"For what?" he said. "Do I know you?" With an easy, loose-hinged walk, he stepped away, not looking back, nodded to the hermaphrodite, then disappeared into the darkness.

The masked man beckoned to us. He opened the door, grinning, and we entered a little cubicle with a bed. It was better than we had expected.

"So . . ." Ferris said. "This is it. I always wondered what my last sight would be."

"Could it be me?" I asked, shyly.

I felt a moment of doubt. With her left finger and thumb, Ferris turned my face, and crushed her lips against mine in answer. My senses swam.

"You've never kissed me like that before," I said.

Her eyes sparkled. "I don't think I've ever kissed *anyone* like that."

"Why?" I asked. "Why here? Why now?"

"There's a last time for everything." Her answer made sense. Everything made sense.

She put the tablet on the end of her tongue, swallowed. She took mine out of my hand, and placed it on the tip of her tongue as well, then kissed me again. I felt it pass from her mouth to mine, and I swallowed it.

Her eyes glowed. "And that's half of it," she said. "Now the rest."

She shed her clothes, the body I knew so well still a revelation, in the dim light so transparent she seemed made of wax. She drew me closer, stroking until I was erect, and then rolled me on top of and into her.

She arched and groaned, pulling at me, and I felt a sensation like being sucked down a deep and endless hole . . .

Her eyes rolled back.

And back . . .

Until they were blood-red spheres without sclera or irises. Tiny black lines against the red. Her mouth opened wider. Wider than any human's had ever opened. There came a sound, barely at the edge of hearing, like an invisible insect fluttering madly within her left ventricle. I couldn't breathe. Were the drugs killing us? Was this entire thing a trap?

I tried to pull out of her, fought to escape, and could not. Her vaginal muscles held me like a vise. I beat at her, smashed my fists against her face until my hands bled . . . and then some other light-colored fluid began streaming from her mouth.

From somewhere deep inside her chest, words arose: *Don't be afraid.*

As consciousness faded, I could hear feet outside, and screaming. The trill of shock-guns. Then silence, and darkness.

*　　*　　*

Darkness receded like an oiled ocean.

I drifted in and out of nausea, briefly finding a clear space, then suddenly passed through another wave of dizziness that washed over me, leaving me weak, feeling first overheated, then chilled. Blinking, I saw the ceiling of a white-tiled medical room. Then I looked down at myself. Naked. My wrists and ankles cuffed to a hospital bed with chrome knobs and metal railing. On a table next to me was a lump covered with dull coppery hair. Ferris's head, disconnected from her body. Her eyes were still filled with bloody liquid, flashing black lines floating within.

I screamed myself hoarse.

The door slid open, and a brown-skinned woman in a white coat, with raven-black hair, eyes green as kelp, and full, bee-stung lips, entered. "Hello, Shane."

She ignored my silence. "How are you feeling? I don't really have to ask that. We have scans, of course, and you're doing fine."

At last, I found my voice and pointed at the severed head. "What is *that*?"

"Your lady love," the woman in the white smock said. "We built ten Ferrises in all, but this one was constructed specifically for you."

"Why?" I asked. "Why *me*?"

The doctor, an Upper in bearing and enunciation, fiddled with dials on a panel. Beams of laser light lanced from the ceiling, mapping and exploring my naked body.

"Oh, I don't mind telling you, because you won't remember." Her voice was mesmerizing, with the faintest of accents and a lilt on her labials. It was like an old, old coin that had traversed continents and civilizations, picking up hard-won knowledge from each one, passed down through centuries, and bearing the palm oil and wisdom of millions who'd handled it: the voice of the polis, enveloping and inescapable. Helplessly, I listened as she said, "We tolerate the boutique death brothels. We look the other way because they help to monitor and regulate deviancy. But a few citizens had disappeared, their microsynthes deactivated and bodies presumably destroyed. The most we could discover was a rumor that Billy was selling an . . . *extreme* form of the drug Thanadose. We hadn't been able to find him, so we began searching out his crèchemates, on the theory that one of them would know how to find him. You were the third one, you know."

"And Ferris . . . was she always . . . ?"

"Yes," the doctor said. "A sex doll reconfigured for analysis. The minute we knew we had the genuine sample, we raided. Now we can reconfigure the microsynthes to compensate."

"Is Billy . . ."

She looked shocked. "Dead? Oh, heavens no. We waste nothing. Like you, he belongs to all of us. And we care about everyone. We always have everyone's best interests in mind. We need him. We need you. I suspect that's something you forgot." All of a sudden, she smiled at a remembrance. "My Caregiver once had a saying I've always seen as wise. 'A place for everything, and everything in its place.'"

A sound breathed through the room, and I finally recognized it. *No way out. No way out* . . . It was my own voice. At some point I had curled against the wall, holding my knees. Rocking.

"Come now," she said brightly. "You've been given a gift for which kings and pharaohs would have gladly exchanged their crowns."

"I don't want it."

"What you—or any of us—want isn't important. We're all essential parts of the whole. Of the city-state. The clan. The family. And it is the height of selfishness to see oneself as separate or special within that collective. That's what brought the old world to an end, you know: the delusion of individuality and personal identity. Of individual nation-states rather than a united polis. It is far, far better to embrace and maintain a well-tuned harmony and tidiness that leads to happiness and security for all. That way, everyone's life contributes to the symphony."

"But I'm *not* happy."

"I know." She smiled, her eyes softening with what I could only call pity. "You were filled with the illusion of yourself. This is a cause for concern, but not alarm, because I can take away some of those disturbing thoughts by removing certain proteins from your amygdala, and regrooving certain chemical pathways and adjusting memory traces."

That was the moment real panic hit me. *"No!"* Then my voice became a whimper. "No . . . They're all I have. They're all of me that's left. All that's *mine.*"

"There *is* no you or me. No mine or yours," she said, and shone a violet light into my eyes. "Only we." Slowly, the edges of my visual field began to burn away.

We waste nothing. Her words. Billy's words. Was he . . . ? But what sense . . . ? I couldn't think, couldn't trust my own memory . . .

Couldn't trust anything . . .

* * *

Shane awakened at home, although it took him a time to determine where he was. He looked at his hands. Pulsing stretches of pinkish, puckered flesh crested the knuckles. Wounded flesh, already knitting together. When had he harmed them? He could not remember.

He dressed, ate, looked around. A rectangular spot on the wall opposite his dining table was slightly discolored, as if a rectangular object had once been positioned there. There used to be something else there, he was certain of it, but could not remember what it was.

Shane took the solotube to work, passing the parks and the ponds, gazing at the distant towers without curiosity. Strange, he thought. He had the sense that once upon a time he had wondered about those towers. Now he did not. If ever he had.

He sat at his place on the Möbius line, just as a broken harp trundled into sight. He examined it and sent it on. The next job was more interesting. And then . . . a plastic woman,

147

in two pieces, body and head. Skin soft and perfect. Dark brown hair as fine as silk. Broken and chipped as if someone had beaten it horribly.

He checked its speech synthesizer, the work of a moment to trigger its last words.

"Don't be afraid," it said.

He shrugged. Wrote out a ticket, and sent it on to the cybernetics track. Just another job, like the job he had done yesterday, and would do tomorrow, and tomorrow, and tomorrow.

A society must work perfectly. Everything in its place.

He noticed that fluid was leaking from the sex doll's damaged eye. In the overhead light, at just the wrong angle, it looked very like a tear.

The Night Belongs
to Phoenix Jones[1]

Got a Jones: to be a
    superhero:
Rise like a phoenix
Fight like De Niro
Knock me down
Like the party crashes
I'll be back
Rising from the ashes.
Super duper hero
I'm more than a zero
Don't need to break my
    nose

Because I'm Seattle's
    own Phoenix Jones
I don't need my own
    Professor X
To make my brain cells
Or muscles flex
Need a villain to be a
    superhero
Someone show the
    world
I'm more than just a
    zero.

—Seattle rock band Quickie, "Phoenix Jones"

I have a secret to share about one of Seattle's newest super-heroes. But it's already getting dark, so I better speak quickly.

Sometimes I used to feel I was the zero in that song about

Phoenix Jones. He was an American hero, and his ongoing saga maybe more uniquely American than even he knows. But I'll get to that in a minute since, as I said, I don't have much time. When I was a kid I loved comic books. I knew all the fantastic adventure heroes, and I revered the writers and artists who created them. But as I got older, what happens to everyone happened to me. My parents and grown-ups told me comic books were childish, and that I should put away childish things and be serious. So I lost my innocence. I became jaded and grown-up and cynical. But it was when I started teaching that I gradually began to see how the grown-ups had been wrong, because the culture of comic book geeks unexpectedly went mainstream. Movies and TV shows became the poor man's literature, our common coin, and all our conversational references came from pop culture. In other words, America had become an amusement society, like ancient Rome. I once asked my students, "Do you see what's happening? Whenever I mention a classic work of fiction, you all shake your heads because none of you have read it, but if I mention a movie, almost all of you have seen it." One of my more honest students raised his hand and said, "Well, sure. It just takes a couple of hours to watch a movie, but it might take a whole week to read a book." He might have added that comic books and graphic novels took even less time than that. Hollywood producers were well aware of this. They figured out that the vast, subversive subculture of costumed characters in seven-by-ten-inch comic books was potentially a trillion-dollar megafun franchise. Comic book conventions, called Comic-Cons, were attended by thousands of grown-ups dressed like their favorite characters. I wondered: Does anyone dress up like Bigger Thomas or Humbert Humbert? Were there action figures and video games for Alexander Portnoy or Rabbit Angstrom or Leopold Bloom? You know the answer to that. The public really didn't hunger for stories about angst-ridden, dryasdust people doing dull things in a dull way. But every kid and even college professors knew a fictional hero like Batman, who is our modern equivalent to myths like Sisyphus. Like Odysseus.

Like Phoenix Jones.

At eight P.M. on October 8, 2011, a Saturday, he came with his posse into the Dreaming,[2] a comic book store at 5226 University Way NE, where I was doing research, to change out of his street clothes and into his $10,000 black-and-gold costume.[3] We were surrounded on all sides of the room with endless titles and garish covers that reminded me of newspaper stands in the 1940s loaded down with pulp magazines about The Shadow and Doc Savage. But, no, I didn't see his face because he was already wearing that mask of his, showing only his eyes and bearded chin.

The owner of the shop saw my face hanging open in surprise. He laughed. "You didn't know he sometimes changes into costume here?"

"I guess I thought he changed in a phone booth."

I only vaguely heard what else he said, because here in the flesh was Seattle's homegrown vigilante and paladin. And, unlike the comic book heroes of my childhood, his flesh was *real*. According to reports I'd read, and rumors I'd heard, that black flesh had been stabbed in Seattle, shot in Tacoma,[4] hit with a baseball bat, and had its nose broken in Belltown. He was a big noise in the real-life superhero movement, someone who claimed he had helped SPD make 253 arrests, and the *Seattle Weekly* said he'd been arrested himself forty-one times, sued twenty-seven times,[5] and spent many nights in county holding cells because of his crusade. His image was all over the Internet, an international meme, and because of that other real-life superheroes around the country—and there were more of these people who put on costumes to help out in soup kitchens and visit sick kids in hospitals than you might imagine—*those* people complained that Phoenix was a glory whore who probably would wind up on a slab with tags on his toes. And, yes, I should mention that sometimes the police felt he kept turning up like a bad penny and wished he'd go away.

He had just come from his second workout of the day at Gold's Gym, where he did sprint-jog intervals on the treadmill. I could see he was buff, a balls-to-the-wall athlete. With him were costumed people named Pitch Black, Ghost, and Black Knight,[6] all armed, each according to his or her fancy.

Somehow I worked up the courage to say, "Can I ride along with you and your crew tonight?"

Phoenix swung his head and looked at me steadily. "You're not another reporter, are you?" His voice was bronze, as befits a superhero.

"Uh, no," I said. "I'm a teacher at Highline Community College. I'm trying to write a monograph on the enormous influence of comic books on popular culture. Sometimes I also do assignments for the *Weekly*."

"You came to the right person then." He was pulling on his bullet-resistant gloves while listening to the police scanner in his cowl, which also has a built-in radio, PA system, and a camera attached to one side. "I'm the first superhero to come along and come as close to a comic book as possible. I'm interesting and I'm charismatic on camera, off camera, and in person."[7] He raised his arms to let Amber, his good-looking girlfriend, adjust his Kevlar neck-piece and leg armor. "You're lucky. You caught us at the right time. I'm a weekend superhero.[8] I only go out on patrol Thursday through Sunday so I can spend the other nights at home with my family." Now Amber helped him squeeze into the ceramic and titanium chest piece he wore over his fire-resistant undershirt, then strap on a utility belt that had a Taser nightstick, pepper spray, and a first-aid kit. "But here's the deal," he said. "You can't reveal my alter ego, who I really am, because I have to protect my loved ones. Agreed?"

I nodded. "Agreed."

So, in short, that's how I found myself tagging along with members of the Rain City Superhero Movement and a documentary filmmaker on a night that would collapse into chaos. When we stepped outside to their car, a Kia sedan,[9] I felt the chill of night air, so cold and crisp, take hold of me. I sat in the backseat beside Phoenix as another Rain City superhero, Midnight Jack, drove, the tocking rhythm of wipers on the windshield and gray music of light rain filling the space between my questions as we cruised over to Capitol Hill, looking for trouble.

I asked him, "Why do you do this?"

He paused for a few seconds to pull his thoughts together.

"All this started when a thief smashed my car window with a rock stuffed inside a ski mask. I kept the mask, and the next night when a fight broke out between two of my friends and some others guys, I put the mask on and chased down the guy who started the fight.[10] So what? So this: I'm asking you to stop letting other people with bad intentions control you. I'm asking *you* to take your streets, neighborhoods, cities, and states back.[11] I'm asking you to let people know you've got their back *just because* . . . Criminals feel free to just run wild in my city, and I'm not going to stand for it."[12]

I was taking notes as fast as I could. But to me Phoenix still seemed like a mystery wrapped inside an enigma. Added to that, there was something very unsettling about talking to someone hiding behind a mask. With his face and expressions concealed this way, I felt he—maybe even *I*—might be capable of doing *any*thing, like a bank robber in a black balaclava, a hooded member of the KKK, or a porn star before 1960 half-hidden behind a carnival mask. Then, suddenly, I had a lightbulb moment: Maybe I was *already* wearing a mask. And you, too. The meaning of everything was always hidden in masquerade. And maybe we all were playing characters, roles, social masks we tried to live up to with identity being both

malleable and imagined. Sometimes that social construct—
the self—felt like a cage. I wondered: What if we took off our
masks, and discovered there was only a bottomless emptiness
and freedom? Was that what we were afraid of?

Midnight Jack parked the car on a side street on Capitol
Hill. I felt I was still scratching at the surface of Phoenix Jones,
but once we started walking down Broadway, with the sharp
odor of marijuana hanging in the air, and Phoenix's eyes track-
ing left, then right for trouble, I discovered there *was* a method
to this madness. To his crime-fighting skills. Flanked by Ghost
and Pitch Black, he stepped up to two heavily tattooed bikers
arguing outside a bar. He told them, "Let's keep it cool, gentlemen, let's all have a good night." The bikers stopped and gaped
in disbelief, as if Phoenix had just fallen from the moon. Or
maybe they thought the circus had just come to town. Twenty
feet away, a coke dealer with Medusa-like dreadlocks stopped
in the middle of a sale, shoving his plastic baggie back into his
pocket. It was as if they'd just seen Pope Francis step out of a
limousine. And then everyone was asking for his autograph,
or for Phoenix to pose with them for a selfie they'd post later
on Facebook. Other people—a generation raised on comic
books and cartoons—came pouring out of restaurants and
taverns to give him a high five, thank him for handing out
food to the homeless, for stopping car and bus jackings and
people urinating in public, and helping tipsy ladies get a cab
at two in the morning. He couldn't swing across Seattle on
a spider's web. Or leap tall buildings in a single bound. But

they knew he was as close as they would ever get to a bona fide costumed crime fighter. Of course, some people heckled him, some threw beer cans at his head, some gave him their middle fingers, and told him to get a life. But for just this moment the shock of seeing him wiped away for a heartbeat any thought anyone had of doing something wrong. He was fun. A free Disneyland distraction. And, to do him justice, wasn't that all anyone ever needed to turn people away from crime—just this *one* present moment in time—for what other moment was there?—to forget themselves and laugh and walk away from trouble with an outrageous story to tell their friends?

Unfortunately, that moment was going to be short-lived.

Phoenix reveled in the adulation of his fans, that was clear. Because he was always thinking of the optics, he posed with them for fifteen minutes. But I could tell he was disappointed that we hadn't yet captured any criminals. It was a slow night for superheroing. He flicked a fast look my way and sighed. "When there's nothing going on, you feel pretty silly in this outfit."[13] His voice sounded flat, a little tired. "Let's patrol on foot a little longer, maybe over on First Avenue."

Back in the car, I asked him if the rumor was true that he was an amateur mixed martial artist and cage fighter. He was silent so I asked him another question. Was he a day-care worker during the day, as some people said, teaching life skills to autistic children? He answered quickly, "Yeah, I love those kids. They're neglected. They're ignored."[14]

Then he left another silence, which I did not break. A

moment passed, then two. His eyes became thoughtful. Then he cleared his throat and lowered his voice by half. "When I was a kid, my whole biological family for some reason or another decided that I wasn't worth anything, so they sent me far away to foster homes. I had thirty brothers and sisters, depending on the time.[15] Everything I had was secondhand. Used. My clothes. My toys. There was nothing I could call my own. I always wanted my piece of something."[16] Phoenix continued, "I've always been poor—evicted twice[17]—but if I have to be an at-risk, young black man, then I want to choose my risks myself. I want them to help other people.[18] When it's all over, I want there to be an account of things that I've done and for people to look at me and say, 'He succeeded. I don't care if people didn't want him. He made himself.' "[19]

I let that sink in. He. Made. Himself. That made me look at *my*self. I could put everything I'd ever done on a three-by-five index card.

It was 2:15 A.M. With little traffic at that hour, we were downtown in ten minutes. And no sooner than Midnight Jack cranked off the ignition, we heard peals of laughter and a commotion outside a nightclub. Faraway liquid figures under the Alaskan Way Viaduct were shouting, darting in and out of darkness.

"Phoenix, look *down*. Look *down*!" Black Knight pointed toward Columbia Street. "Big fight!"[20]

Phoenix sprinted from the car, tearing full tilt toward them, holding two cans of pepper spray, shouting back over his shoulder in a voice shredded by the wind, "Go, go, go! Get me nine-one-one! Call nine-one-one!"

That's when everything spun out of control.

When I caught up with the others, my chest pounding, Phoenix was bellowing at a group of people, "Break it up!" Enraged, a woman began pounding wildly on him with her shoe, hurtling words like stones. "You piece of shit!" Then, as it happened, she tripped and fell flat on her face. Out of nowhere, a silver car came plowing down the wrong side of the road on Western Avenue, nearly hitting one of the partygoers. Young men were lunging at Phoenix, who pepper-sprayed one of them in the face. He threw me a look of panic. "Where are the cops? We need the cops *now*. This is getting serious. Protect yourselves." I was feeling panicky myself, but, so help me, the rush of adrenaline made me feel buoyant, too.

The woman who fell was shouting, "I got fucking pepper spray in my eye!"

Behind me, the documentary filmmaker, who had been following Phoenix for eight months, was sputtering into his cell phone. "There's a huge group of people fighting at Columbia and Western, and there's pepper spray, and superheroes, and I don't know . . ."

To me, the police didn't so much arrive as they seemed to materialize out of thin air. The woman who fell would later identify herself as Maria on radio station KING 5, saying, "We were just walking down to our parking lot after having a good time in Seattle, when a little argument broke out between our group and another group, and all of sudden we were attacked by these guys wearing Halloween costumes." She demanded that Phoenix be arrested. The cops were more than happy to comply. They took away his cans of pepper spray. One officer glared at me and others in the Rain City crew. "Anybody *else* want to join this party? We're about to arrest the whole bunch of ya and clean things up. We're about tired of this game."

I watched them clamp handcuffs on Phoenix. Then lead him to a patrol car. Inside, he sat with his shoulders hunched, his head slung forward. Then his eyes swung up, and he gave me a sheepish sideways look. "I guess it's been a long day's night, eh?"[21]

He was in King County Jail for the next seven hours, arrested on suspicion of fourth-degree assault.[22] They took away his super suit, telling him, "This way we can keep your big mouth shut." That afternoon, after posting a $3,800 bail with no charges filed, he was all over the news again. Two days later he was in court with his lawyer. I was there watching with members of the Rain City Superhero Movement, feeling for the first time like I was one of them.

A court officer made him take off his mask during the hearing. When he did I clapped both hands over my mouth to muffle my reaction. No, he wasn't bad-looking. Just not how I imagined he might look. He didn't have chiseled features or a lantern jaw. But his hair *was* dramatic, an imitation of the do worn by a popular, early 1990s hip-hop performer named Christopher "Kid" Reid. It looked like a black pencil eraser on top of his head. And during the proceedings, he saddled his nose with a pair of wimpy spectacles that even Clark Kent wouldn't wear. But now the world knew his name, Benjamin Fodor. That he was twenty-three years old. And that he had a 5-2 amateur mixed martial arts record, fighting under the name—wait for it—Flattop.

You'd think that would have been the end of the adventures of Phoenix Jones. He did lose his day-care job. But being unmasked opened new doors. The offers came pouring in, even from Hollywood. He went from amateur to pro when he signed a contract with the World Series of Fighting, and won his first match in three minutes against Roberto Yong on September 18, 2015. One day later, he stopped an attempted murder on Capitol Hill.[23]

It's almost midnight. I've graded all my students' papers for tomorrow after spending hours correcting their grammar. That would be unbearable if it wasn't for what I do now in the wee hours of morning. My skintight Spandex costume, just back from the cleaners and very sexy, hangs in my closet, waiting for me. Friday, Saturday, and Sunday nights still belong to Phoenix Jones.

But Monday through Thursday belong to me.

Notes

1 Because Phoenix Jones is a real, living person whom I respect and admire, and also because I had to take a certain degree of artistic license in this fictional story about him, I think providing endnotes

for my sources as well as pointing out what I've invented for literary reasons is appropriate.

For information about Phoenix Jones, I relied on published news stories, his online posts, YouTube videos, and the following book interviews and articles: Jon Ronson, *The Amazing Adventures of Phoenix Jones* (Riverhead Books, 2011); Keegan Hamilton, "The (Alleged) Adventures of Phoenix Jones," *Seattle Weekly,* June 1–7, 2011; Nick Wong, "Phoenix Jones: Portrait of a Superhero," fightland .vice.com/blog/phoenix-jones-portrait-of-a-superhero, April 6, 2015; Stephie Haynes, "Phoenix Jones: Getting to Know the Man Behind the Mask," www.bloodyelbow.com/, March 28, 2015; and Ryan McNamee Productions and Phoenix Jones, "Phoenix Jones Stops Assault on Vimeo," http://vimeo.com, October 10, 2011.

2 There is a photo of Phoenix Jones and superhero Buster Doe in the Dreaming comics and game store, which accompanies Ashby Jones's story "Bam! Pow! Superhero Groups Clash over Roles, Methods," *Wall Street Journal,* February 25, 2011. However, I have no idea if Phoenix Jones visited the Dreaming on October 8, 2011.

3 This expensive, elaborate version of Phoenix Jones's super suit came, I believe, later when he had a fund-raising campaign to upgrade his costume, http://the phoenixjones.blogspot.com/, August 15, 2015.

4 Hamilton, "(Alleged) Adventures," p. 13.

5 Catherine Avalone, "Randall Beach: The Bloody and Often Odd Life of a 'Superhero,'" *New Haven Register,* posted April 4, 2015.

6 Those are real-life superheroes, but I don't know who was with Phoenix Jones on this night of his arrest.

7 Hamilton, "(Alleged) Adventures," p. 12.

8 Avalone, "Randall Beach," p. 4.

9 Hamilton, "(Alleged) Adventures," reports seeing Phoenix Jones in a Kia sedan, but I doubt he was driving that on this night.

10 Ibid., p. 11.

11 http://thephoenixjones.blogspot.com/.

12 Christina Ng, "Citizen Superhero 'Phoenix Jones' Arrested in Seattle," *Good Morning America,* http://abcnews.go.com/US/citizen-superhero -phoenix-jones-arrested-seattle/story?id=14704985.

13 Jones, "Bam! Pow!"

14 Wong, "Phoenix Jones," p. 14.

15 Ibid., p. 10.

16 Ibid., p. 11.

17 Hamilton, "(Alleged) Adventures)," p. 16.
18 The rest of this sentence is my imagined dialogue for Phoenix Jones.
19 Wong, "Phoenix Jones," p. 11.
20 This entire scene is taken from McNamee Productions and Jones, "Phoenix Jones Stops Assault."
21 This line about a "long day's night" was the theme or creative prompt given to writers Claudia Castro Luna, Nancy Horan, and myself when we agreed to write new stories for the seventeenth Bedtime Stories literary gala sponsored by Humanities Washington on October 2, 2015. For these events, the theme must appear somewhere in the story.
22 Sara Jean Green, "Superhero Bound for Court," *Seattle Times,* p. B1.
23 "Phoenix Jones Stops Attempted Murder," *King County News,* September 23, 2015.

Night Hawks

कर्मण्येवाधिकारस्ते
मा फलेसु कदाचन
मा कर्मफलहेतुर् भुर्
मा ते सङ्गो ऽस्त्व् अकर्मणि

Your right is to action alone; never to its fruits
at any time. Never should the fruits of action be
your motive; never let there be attachment to
inaction in you.

—Bhagavad Gita, book II, sloka 47

Seven or sevenish

Playwright August Wilson and I always met at 7:00 P.M. at
the Broadway Bar and Grill, which was just a short walk
from his many-roomed home on Capitol Hill in Seattle. We
looked for the smokers' section at the rear of the restaurant in a
spacious, dimly lit room with two televisions mounted on the
peach-colored walls. He would arrive as tidily dressed as ever,

his demeanor courtly and dignified, even gracious, with his
salt-and-pepper goatee neatly trimmed, and wearing a stylish,
plaid cap on his balding head. (He once told me, "I should
just *stop* going to the barbershop.") We were two old men with
a combined hundred-plus years of American history on our
heads, only three years apart in age, and raised in the 1940s
and '50s by proud, hardworking parents. You might say that
for fifteen years these eight- to ten-hour dinner conversations
at the Broadway were our version of a boys' night out. It was a
lively, laid-back place filled with young people, straights and
gays, students and Goths, and much nicer than the dangerous
place we would end up in before this evening was over.

After a handshake and a hug, we would sit down, order
organic Sumatra French Roast coffee and a big plate of chicken
nachos with black beans, olives, and guacamole. Then we
began the ritual that defined for me our friendship. We always
tried to remember to bring some kind of gift for each other.
It was a ritual of respect, generosity, and civility. The pres-
ents we gave each other were always art, or about art, and
each represented our lifelong passion for the creative process.
Because he knew I was a cartoonist and illustrator, he would
give me, say, the tape of a documentary showing Picasso at
work, or *The Complete Cartoons of the New Yorker* and *The
Complete Far Side* by Gary Larson. I, in turn, would give him
a limited-edition, facsimile reproduction of one of Jorge Luis
Borges's short story manuscripts presented to me during a
State Department–sponsored lecture tour in Spain, because

Borges, Amiri Baraka, Romare Bearden, and the blues, or the "Four Bs" as August called them, were the major influences on his work.

Eight o' clock

Finally, after we'd examined and discussed our gifts, and the waiter, a thin young woman, leggy and tattooed, with bright red hair and a nose ring, returned to top off our coffee for the second time, we'd relax and let our hair down. This experience, we both knew, was extremely rare in the lonely, solitary lives of writers, especially those considered to be successful by the way the world judged things, so we sometimes looked at each other as if to say, "How did *you* happen?" This unstated question was filled with equal parts of curiosity and affection, partly because he and I belonged to an in-between, liminal generation that remembered segregation yet was also the fragile bridge to the post–civil rights period and beyond; and partly because American culture had changed so much since we began writing in the 1960s, growing coarser, more vulgar and selfish year by year, distancing itself from the vision of our parents, who were raised to value good manners, promise keeping, personal sacrifice, loyalty to their own parents and kin, and a deep-rooted sense of decency. On the stage, his goal was to make audiences respect their hardscrabble lives and his own. This new era of hip-hop, misogynistic gangsta rap, and profanity-laced ghetto lit sometimes made our souls feel like they needed to take a shower. He told me often that if he ever met the Wayans brothers, he planned on slapping both of them silly.

"You know what?" I could tell by the tilt of his head that he felt playful tonight. "When I was out of town for rehearsal these last few months, I'd leave my hotel room, walk over to the theater, and every day I'd see the same man panhandling on the street. He stopped me every day, and every time he had something new for me, so I had to give him some money. For example, one day he pointed down at my feet, and he said, 'I *know* where you got those good-lookin' shoes. I can *tell* you exactly where you got those fancy shoes.'"

The man August was describing could easily have been an antic character in one of his plays.

"You got 'em on your *feet*," he said. "But I know somethin' else, too. I know the day you were born. I can *tell* you the very day you were born, and I won't be wrong or off by more than three days."

August was born on April 27, 1945.

When he asked this fellow what day he was born, the man cackled and said "Wednesday."

And so it went for fifteen years of pas de deux. Sometimes we'd lean into the table to hear each other better when our voices were blurred by the clatter and clang of dishes and swirl of laughter and conversation from other tables around us, talking about our hopes for our children, our wives, our agents and lawyers and business partners, the next story we planned to write for Humanities Washington's yearly Bedtime Stories fund-raiser, a passage I translated for him that he liked from the Bhagavad Gita and our works in progress—*Gem of the Ocean* and *Radio Golf* for him, the novel *Dreamer* for me. But for the most part, and because I'm Buddhist, I did the lion's share of listening. Also because my middle-class life in the Chicago suburb of Evanston had not been half as hard as his in the Hill District of Pittsburgh. He wanted someone to listen as he spoke about his life, all the experiences and ideas not always in his plays but which were, in fact, the background for his ten-play cycle. Over fifteen years, I heard about his biological father, Frederick Kittel, the German baker who was always absent from his life, and his stepfather, an ex-convict who spent twenty-three years in prison for robbery and murder. He adopted his mother's maiden name, Wilson, in rejection of his German father; he began using his middle name, August, when a friend told him not to let anyone call him by the first name he used throughout childhood, which was Freddie. August told me that when he entered the newly integrated public schools of Pittsburgh, he was attacked by a gang of other kids; the principal had to send him home in a taxicab to protect him, but all he could do was ask over and over, "*Why?* Why are they trying to hurt *me*? What did *I* do?" And I learned about why he dropped out of high school his freshman year when a black teacher accused him of plagiarizing a twenty-page term paper entitled "Napoleon's Will to Power" and refused to apologize.

Out of school at age sixteen, he worked at menial jobs. "I dropped out of high school, not life," he often said, and that was true: he may not have been a formally trained intellectual, but he was an organic one, who read shelf after shelf of books at his local library, and dreamed of becoming a writer. No, he was not in school, but he did have a reliable and constant teacher: suffering. "If you want to be a writer," a prostitute once told him, "then you better learn how to write about *me*." He did take her advice. He also joined the Army, and was doing quite well, but, being a proud and hot-blooded young man, he left when he was told he was still too young to apply for officers' training school. There was a year in his life when he was a member of the Nation of Islam, an organization he joined because he hoped to win back the love of his Muslim wife after she unexpectedly left him, taking their daughter and stripping their home clean of every stick of furniture. Entering those barren rooms, said August, was so devastating and heartbreaking that this shock of emptiness washed the strength from his limbs. How many times had his heart been broken? He could not remember the countless disappointments. Like so many writers and artists I've known, his art was anchored in lacerations and a latticework of scar tissue. All that raw pain, poverty and disappointment, denial and disrespect—-as when critic Robert Brustein said he had "an excellent mind for the twelfth century"—all *this* he alchemized into plays that, before his death in 2005, earned him two Pulitzer Prizes, eight New York Drama Critics' Circle Awards, a Tony Award, an

Olivier Award, a National Humanities Medal presented by Bill Clinton, a Broadway theater renamed in his honor, and twenty-eight honorary degrees.

Yet the public could know only the media-created surface, not the subterranean depths, of any artist. Every time you sat down to create something your soul was at stake. Every page—indeed, every paragraph—had been a risk. Every sentence had been a prayer. So when speaking of those honorary degrees, August told me that he recently came across one of them in his attic and suddenly burst into tears because he couldn't for the life of him remember this particular award that was so dear-bought with his own emotional blood. What no one knew of, or could know, was that after every one of his ten plays opened, he fell into a period of severe depression that always lasted for two solid weeks.

He talked freely because he knew I understood these things, how despite the strong black male personas our past pain made us present to the world, we were far more sensitive than we could ever dare show (and *had* to be sensitive and vulnerable in order to create), with the external world being no more than raw material for our imaginations, and that meant we were eccentric: he didn't drive, or do e-mail, or exercise, and if someone walking a dog came his way on the sidewalk, he would step into the street because dogs frightened him, why I can't say. More than once he shared with me his fantasy of finishing his ten plays and telling the world he was retiring. Then, when the reporters went away, the phone stopped ringing, and he vanished from public view, August planned on sitting on his Capitol Hill porch reading piles of books he never had the time to get to, playing with his young daughter, and writing without interruption or distraction for a decade. When that ten years ended, he said, he planned to emerge from seclusion like Eugene O'Neill after *his* decade away from the spotlight, and with plays that would be as powerful and enduring as *The Iceman Cometh, Long Day's Journey into Night,* and *A Moon for the Misbegotten*. He also hoped one day to write a novel.

Those nights at the Broadway Bar and Grill, he needed to talk about things like this. And sometimes he expressed a fear that shook me to my very foundations.

Midnight

At some point during our conversations his thoughts always turned to the ambiguous state of black America. Like the narrator of Charles Dickens's *A Tale of Two Cities,* you could say for black America that "It was the best of times, it was the worst of times." August and I were doing well, he said, but he couldn't forget the fact that Broadway theater tickets were expensive and 25 percent of black people lived in poverty, and therefore never saw his plays. He said there were too many black babies born out of wedlock and without fathers in their homes. Too many young black men were in prison, or the victims of murder. Too many were living with the HIV virus. It was as if forty years after the end of the Jim Crow era, black America was falling apart.

"So let me ask you a question," he said. We'd long ago finished our entrées (the Dungeness crab sandwich for me, the grilled cedar plank salmon for him) and had lost count of how many times the waiter had filled our coffee cups. The last four hours had passed as if they were only fifteen minutes. Only a sprinkling of people remained in the rear of the Broadway Bar and Grill, which was less noisy now so his voice was clear against the background of music drifting from the front room. "Do you think any of it matters?"

"What?"

"Everything we've done." His eyes narrowed a little and smoke spiraled up his wrist from his cigarette. "Nothing we've done changes or improves the situation of black people. We're still powerless and disrespected every day—by everyone and ourselves. People still think black men are violent and lazy and stupid. They see you and me as the exceptions, not the rule."

"You don't see any real changes since the sixties?"

"No," he said. "Not really."

For a moment I didn't know what to say. I knew he meant all this. You could see it in his plays, that sense of despair, futility, and stasis. If he was right, then I wondered, What *good* was art? And his words took the philosopher in me to an even deeper dread. If you paused for just a moment and pulled back from our minuscule dust mote of a planet in one of a hundred billion galaxies pinwheeling across a 13-billion-year-old universe that one day would experience proton death, then it was certain that all men and women had ever done would one day be as if it never was. I wondered: Had we then wasted our lives? Was man, as Sartre put it in *Being and Nothingness,* "a useless passion"?

Two o'clock

I was about to press him on this point about the social impotence of art and, by virtue of that, ourselves, but now our waiter was standing beside us.

"I'm sorry, but you guys are going to have to go. We need to close."

We paid our bill, left a generous tip, and stepped outside to the empty street, talking on the wide strip of cement for another hour. Both of us realized that this business of whether art mattered beyond the easily forgotten awards and evanescent applause was an issue that had reenergized us—or maybe it was the coffee we'd been drinking for the last seven hours. Also, we both knew it was still too early to go home to our wives. Accordingly, August suggested we find a twenty-four-hour place so we could keep on talking. The only restaurant open was a nearby International House of Pancakes. We climbed into my Jeep Wrangler and drove south on East Broadway to Madison Street, where I hung a left and after one block downshifted into the helter-skelter of a parking lot. Something was wrong here. There was a blue-and-white police car outside IHOP and a cop was talking to one of the employees wearing a gray, short-sleeved shirt and a blue apron. As nearly as I could tell, something had happened just before we arrived, perhaps a robbery, but we didn't know for sure. Confused but not ready to give up on the night, we stepped around the police car and went through the double doors inside.

Three o'clock

The dining area was a brightly lit rectangle with two ceiling fans turning slowly and booths arranged along the walls and down the middle. Unlike the Broadway, the customers in IHOP at this hour were night hawks, the people who slept all day and only ventured out after dark: a group that may have included the occasional prostitute, gangbanger, pimp, or drug dealer. No one seemed to recognize either of us as a famous writer. A fidgety waiter seated us in a booth behind the cash register. I saw the police car pull away. Inside, the air felt tense and fibrous. The other patrons were poker-faced and skittish, speaking in whispers, watching for something, their eyes occasionally flashing with fear. August noticed this, too, but he said nothing. He was more at home in this setting than I was. It was a replay of Pittsburgh's Hill District. He knew what to expect. I didn't. When the waiter brought us two cups of flat, brackish coffee, we tried to resume our conversation, but try as I might, I couldn't concentrate on his words. And what happened next I had not expected. The front doors opened, and two young men wearing lots of bling—the one in front compact in build, the one behind him tall and thin like Snoop Dogg—walked straight past a waiter who tried to seat them, and headed toward a table in the back where two women sat with a chuffy-cheeked young man whose complexion was pitted and pockmarked. The first man, handsome and clean-timbered, with the plucky confidence of the actor Ice Cube, began singing at the man who was seated. But wait. It wasn't singing. It was rap. A kind of rhymed challenge. I couldn't make out the words. Being an old gaffer, I could *never* keep up with the japper of fast-talking rappers, but everyone in IHOP sat listening, frozen in their seats and afraid of this situation. Then he and his companion laughed and walked back to the lobby. A moment later, the man with bad skin stood up, clenching and unclenching his fists, and he walked with long strides to the lobby, too. I could tell they were talking. A few seconds passed. Then all at once I heard a tumult, a crash, a sound of shattering glass. I half stood on the red seat beneath me to see better. The first two men sailed like furies into the third, smashing wooden high chairs over his head. He jackknifed at the waist and I heard a *flump* as he hit the floor. The other two stomped his fingers and kicked his face to a pulp, breaking bone and cartilage. Then they fled. Their victim staggered weakly to his feet, his breath tearing in and out of his chest, blood gushing from his lips. Then he, too, reeled out into the night.

The fight was over in ten seconds. All that time I'd been holding my breath. Finally, I faced round to August. But he was gone. Not too surprisingly, I picked him out in a crowd of customers who had wisely scrambled toward the exit at the back of the room. The moment the fight started, his old Pittsburgh instincts had kicked in, telling him to duck for cover in case someone started shooting.

Four o'clock

It took the police only a few minutes to return to IHOP. The restaurant's manager apologized to the patrons for the incident, which surely would be reported in the next day's *Seattle Times* and seen as just more bad PR for black people. The manager said we didn't have to pay for anything we ordered. We felt shaken by what we'd seen. Forty years earlier, we could have been those young men destroying each other. I looked at him; he looked at me, and perhaps we both thought at the same time, *How did* you *happen?*

It went without saying that we figured it was finally time to go home to our wives and children.

We stepped carefully around pools of blood, broken glass, and splinters of wood at the entrance, and returned to my Jeep in the early morning light, the air full of moisture. I said little. A strong rain wind slammed into the Jeep as I drove him home, making me hunch over the steering wheel. Finally, August broke the silence. He said, "People always ask me why black folks don't go to the theater. I try to tell them we've got *enough* ritual and drama in our lives already."

I stopped my Jeep in front of his house. We shook hands, and promised to get together again soon. Since his death, I often replay in my mind the image of America's most celebrated black playwright slowly climbing the steps to his front door; and at last I understood in what way decades devoted unselfishly day and night to art really mattered. The love of beauty had been our lifelong refuge as black men, a raft that carried us both safely for sixty years across a turbulent sea of violence, suffering, and grief to a far shore we'd never dreamed possible in our youth, one free of fear, and when his journey was over laid him gently, peacefully to eternal rest.

Acknowledgments

I wish to thank Humanities Washington, which over the course of nineteen years has inspired me to compose a new work of short fiction every year for its Bedtime Stories literary gala, eleven of which are included in this book. I am equally grateful to my literary agents of the past forty-four years, Georges and Anne Borchardt; to my agent for speaking engagements, Jodi Solomon; to my outstanding editor for this volume, Kathryn Belden, and to Susan Moldow, Scribner president; to science fiction writer Steven Barnes for our collaborations; to the officers of the Charles Johnson Society at the American Literature Association for their superb critical response to my works; and to all the kind editors who separately published these stories in *StoryQuarterly, Boston Review, The Kenyon Review, Shambhala Sun, The Burning Maiden, Spark,* and *The Iowa Review.*